To Kelly.

From Granny a Grandad.
Lovdet Love 2003

THE TREACLE MINE AFFAIR

The TREACLE MINE Affair

D. E. Tucker

The Book Guild Ltd
Sussex, England

The Book Guild Ltd
25 High Street
Lewes, Sussex

First published 1993

Set in Century Schoolbook

Typesetting by Southern Reproductions (Sussex)
East Grinstead, Sussex

Printed in Great Britain by
Antony Rowe Ltd
Chippenham, Wiltshire

A catalogue record for this book is
available from the British Library

ISBN 0 86332 840 7

CONTENTS

DRAWINGS

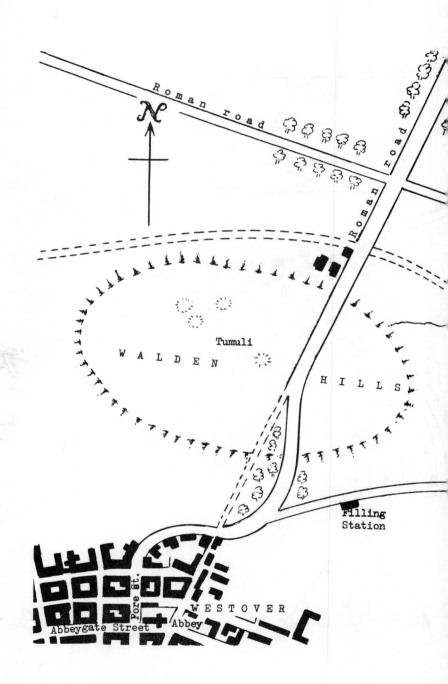

MAP OF
BINCOMBE
Helen Bairstow
delineavit et typoscripsit

Bin Brook

Binbrook
Farm

BINCOMBE
Bincombe
Pool

High Street

Ch.

Beech
House

P.O.

Up-hill
Farm

Meter
House

Springs

Bradbury
Castle

The
Swallock

Walden
Lodge

Quarry

Magpie
Ground

Pond

Timber
yard

Stag-headed
oak

To Market Lydford

Scale of

0   ½   1

M I L E S

1

A Geiger counter

Do you know what a Geiger counter is? And what it looks like? Not everybody does.

You wouldn't expect to find a Geiger counter at a junk-shop in an old-fashioned country town. Quite unexpectedly, Adrian did find one in just such a place.

It was a Friday afternoon in June. Matting had been laid on the concrete strip at the back of the gymnasium, nets erected, and anyone who wished to practise bowling or batting after school could do so. Adrian was not one to miss such an opportunity, and was enjoying the exercise, when he suddenly remembered it was time for him to catch his bus for home.

Bat in hand, he seized his satchel of school books and ran: round the gymnasium, across a cobbled yard, through Saint Michael's Arch, along under the lime trees, past the almshouses. Now he was nearing the middle of the ancient town. The Jubilee Clock in the Market Place told him he had only two minutes left. This sunny afternoon there were people, prams and motor vehicles everywhere; in his hurry they all seemed to be in his way.

Adrian was getting his second wind when he passed the Abbey and swung round into Fore Street.

There it happened. He started to run across the pedestrian crossing, for the bus stop was just up the road on the far side. As he did so a fast-moving sports car came from the right. Adrian stopped short in his tracks. At that

9

moment his cricket bat caught in the grating of a road gully, throwing him off his balance. He escaped being knocked down by the car but stumbled back on a baby's pram, dragging its handles to the ground and its front wheels into the air. The mother screamed.

You seldom met a policeman on foot patrol in Westover, but today as Adrian struggled to his feet he found himself confronted by a constable.

'Assault and battery, my boy; that's what I'll have to book you for,' the bobby said.

Adrian wasn't sure if he was joking. 'It was that sports car – it nearly ran me over,' he protested. But the constable had turned his attention to the young woman with the pram and the baby in it, who to Adrian's relief was not crying but seemed rather to have enjoyed being jolted.

The Bincombe bus went by on the other side of the road.

'Sorry!' Adrian gasped to the young woman. Then, ignoring the policeman, he grabbed his scattered possessions, and making sure this time that the road was clear he darted over the crossing and ran for the bus stop. He could see his sister Helen getting on the bus. He waved his bat and shouted to her to hold the bus until he could catch up, but she did not see or hear him. His final spurt was unsuccessful; he saw the bus pull away from its stopping-place and watched it disappear in the distant traffic.

Adrian had an hour to wait for the next bus and pondered how to spend it. He dared not recross the road and retrace his steps to the school for fear of meeting the policeman again; the bobby might still want his name and address or give him an unwelcome talking-to. Instead Adrian wandered down Fore Street on the same side, mingling with the shoppers and tourists.

The shop called Aladdin's Cave always attracted him. It was a shop with a difference. The sign board was painted in gaudy pseudo-Oriental characters, more Chinese-looking than Arabic, and below it was a notice that said

'Let Aladdin clear your house. Prices better than auction'. The resulting bric-à-brac crowded the shop and spilled out on to the pavement.

Aladdin was selective about what he displayed outside. Today there were two tatty armchairs and a kitchen table loaded with dusty books, gramophone records and cracked crockery. 'If yer leave fings scullin' arahnd wivaht yer mince-pies on 'em, yer'll 'ave 'em nicked,' he once remarked. 'But I don't mind if dem fings ahtside is pinched.'

Behind the plate-glass windows, however, was a feast of surprises. Adrian saw a gilded weather-cock, looking unexpectedly large when seen close up, and leaning drunkenly against it a wind-doll painted like a grenadier guard; they might have come out of somebody's garden. Adrian let his eyes wander to two silver trumpets grouped with a piano accordion, an electric guitar, a big bass drum and an American reed organ. On the organ rested a miniature sailing-ship in a glass bottle, an ivory chess set, a stainless-steel model of Stephenson's *Rocket* and a Morse sending key with trailing wires still attached to its brass terminals.

There must have been children in the houses that Aladdin had cleared, for Adrian noticed a fully furnished doll's house, a Hornby train set and a toy fort with cannon and a company of battle-scarred lead soldiers. Behind the fort stood a rocking-horse, its head blinkered by a shiny brass fireman's helmet.

Aladdin's Cave had already yielded Adrian some useful trophies, including a waterproof electric torch and a pair of eight-by-forty binoculars, just right for bird-watching. He was wondering now whether to go into the shop and explore its remote cavities, when his attention was caught by the sound of a motor vehicle drawing up behind him. It was the sports car that had nearly run him down, a vintage Perugi Six reconditioned and resplendent in polished black enamel and chromium plating. Now it was towing a green-painted horse trailer. Two men got out, the driver

11

and his passenger.

Later Adrian remembered that the driver was tall and thin, slightly stooping, with a sallow face, fuzzy black hair and a toothbrush moustache; he was dressed in a smart grey suit and pink shirt and tie. His companion was short, rather plump and beer-bellied, with a round head, short-cropped hair, ruddy face, large red nose and a gingery moustache; he was wearing jeans and an open-necked shirt covered by a white cotton-drill coat.

As the driver came round the front of the car he knocked over a bicycle propped against the kerb. Without stopping, he and the stout man strode into the junk-shop.

Adrian recognized the bicycle as belonging to one of his schoolfellows, but its owner was nowhere in sight. He picked it up, checked that it was not damaged, and propped it up against the kerb again where nobody would fall over it.

He noticed that the Perugi Six had a London registration, ALE 9876, an old one that did not really tell where its present owner came from. He noticed also that the vehicle licence had expired on the 30th April. He peered into the horse trailer but could see no animal inside.

Now Adrian too went into Aladdin's Cave, for a small object in the window had caught his eye.

The two men from the car were having some sort of dispute with Aladdin. Adrian knew that Aladdin's real name was George Smith, and he came not from the Middle East but from the East End of London. Aladdin spoke in a lively manner.

'Sorry, gents,' Adrian heard him say, 'but if yer can't back yer cheque wif a bank card, doancher see, I can't take it.'

There was more discussion, then the tall man pulled out a bank note from a pocket and apparently the purchase was made, for Adrian heard him say, 'All right, then. We'll take it now.'

The item referred to was a dumpy metal cylinder fitted

with a large burner and tripod. Adrian had examined it on a previous visit, and he remembered reading a dog-eared label attached to it that read:

TYER'S OIL FURNACE:
Used by electricians, cable joiners, water and gas engineers, plumbers &c. Will melt solder, lead, tin, bitumen, pitch &c. Size No 4. Melts 56 lb metal &c.

The man in the white coat struggled to lift the cylinder, the tall man cautiously took hold of the burner as though he did not wish to soil his suit. Aladdin put a strong arm round the tripod to help them to the shop door and out into the sunshine. The tailboard of the horse trailer had to be let down, and there was a further struggle to load the Tyer's oil furnace inside. Then the tailboard was lifted back and clamped tight, the two men climbed into the Perugi and they drove off.

In Aladdin's Cave the item that had caught Adrian's interest was an object of metal, glass and plastic, about the size of a wine glass. He had seen something like it on television, but too fleetingly to take in details. When Aladdin came back into his Cave, Adrian asked him what it was.

'I dunno, chum.'

'Where did it come from, then?'

'Well, nah, vat's somefin' I can't tell yer.'

It flashed through Adrian's mind that whatever it was had been stolen, but Aladdin's next words reassured him.

'Yer see, I got a pal. 'E goes an' buys fings. Big stuff, yer see: electric motors, power tools, anyfin' like vat. Sometimes bankrup' stock, or it might be all v' machines in some fact'ry vats closin' dahn. Once it was some big science lavatory. Anyfing vat's not 'is line, yer see, 'e passes on ter me. Vat's 'ow I come by vat fing.'

'Does it work?' Adrian asked.

13

'I dunno.'

'And you really don't know what it is?'

'Well, I reckon it might be somefin' electric-like.'

'I don't really know what it is myself,' Adrian admitted, 'but my friend Sparky Harris might know. He's been in the Navy and he's a wizard with anything electrical.'

'D'yer want ter buy it, ven?'

'It all depends on how much you want for it.'

There was a pause. Adrian looked the little object over to see if there were any cracks. Eventually he decided to risk a week's pocket money but no more, and made an offer accordingly. His offer was accepted – much to his surprise, for if the thing really was a Geiger counter, as he hoped, it would be worth much more than that.

By chance Adrian had just enough money on him to pay Aladdin forthwith. Then, putting his purchase in a pocket, he gathered up his cricket bat and satchel of books and made once more for the Bincombe bus. This time he caught it.

As the bus climbed the winding road out of Westover and up the hill beyond, he could see that hay-making had started in meadows on either side. At one stage the bus had to crawl along behind a tractor-drawn wagon piled high as a house with bales of hay, but at last the road straightened and the bus-driver signalled to following traffic that he was about to overtake the hay wagon. He started to pull out from the nearside lane and pressed down on his accelerator pedal. As he did so there was an impatient blast from a motor horn; a shiny black sports car shot forward from behind and raced past with noisy exhaust.

Instinctively the bus-driver steered back into the nearside lane to avoid being hit by the overtaking car. At that instant the tractor-driver changed gear and momentarily lost speed. The bus-driver braked and his passengers were jerked forward, but the front of the bus caught the tail of the wagon. The load of hay swayed.

Adrian again recognized the Perugi Six he had

encountered earlier; now without the horse trailer, it was moving fast and in seconds disappeared beyond a rise in the road ahead.

The bus-driver resignedly waved on the traffic queuing behind him and stopped to see what damage had been done. The tractor-driver, who had felt a jolt, stopped also. Adrian knew him slightly: he was Denny, brother of Danny, his father's farm worker. He had the same gangling limbs as his brother, the same mop of wavy black hair, the same rosy face and very blue eyes.

Fortunately the trailer was strongly built, the hay bales were well tied on with new ropes, and nothing had tipped over. The impact had been partly cushioned by the hay, and damage to both bus and trailer was no more than scratches.

'I doan't blame 'ee,' said Denny to the busman. 'It's these yer smarty-boots what tries to pull fast 'uns over honest folks like we.'

They parted with no ill feeling.

The bus continued along the straight road, a highway laid out by Romans nearly two thousand years before; then, at a crossing, it swung into a narrower road signposted to Bincombe. The journey should have taken less than fifteen minutes, but now the bus was late. At stopping-places passengers got off in ones and twos; some were met by relatives, some waved to acquaintances. Adrian knew most of them, but Sparky Harris was not among them.

He himself got off at Bincombe Post Office Stores and turned into the lane leading to Up-hill Farm. He trod this lane in each direction almost every day, so knew it well. On a gate pillar as he turned the corner he saw Anthracite, the Doctor's shiny black tom-cat, dreamily basking. The Doctor's spreading copper beech just beyond was now in full leaf, but fading candles of blossom on the horse chestnuts that made an avenue at the foot of the hill reminded Adrian that springtime was already passing, that summer holidays were only a month away, and that his

15

cousins Robin and Peg would then be joining him and
Helen at Bincombe. Higher up the lane, umbels of cow
parsley were bowing low, already heavy with seeds, but red
campion still stood upright in full bloom, glowing in the
late-afternoon sunshine, and the hedgerows were swollen
with billows of elder-flowers.

Adrian's home was half a mile up the lane, which
steepened and narrowed as he proceeded. Although the
lane was not heavily trafficked – knotgrass and mayweed
grew thinly along its middle – it had been cut deeply into
the hillside here by centuries of wear and rainfall long
before the invention of tarred macadam, so the hedges on
either side were now left standing on high banks. The
hedge on Adrian's right was an old one of mixed
blackthorn and a dozen other kinds of shrub; it might have
been planted by the monks of Byncume about the time of
the Domesday survey. On his left was a beech hedge
bordering the Walden Lodge estate; it had not been cut for
many years, so the beeches were grown tall and were
mixed with ash and sycamore saplings, sprouted from
winged seeds and fast assuming the stature of forest trees.
The neglected woodland behind was full of wild birds and
nestlings. Adrian noticed a cuckoo wavering over the tree
tops with shallow beats of his pointed wings, singing his
unceasing call even in flight.

As Adrian approached Up-hill Farm the hedge on his
right had a very different and cared-for appearance; it had
been cut and laid the previous winter by his father and
Danny, the general farm worker, and now in full leaf was
proof against the most wayward of farm animals.

Shep, the black-and-white Border collie, heard Adrian's
approach and leapt over the stone garden wall, waving his
big tail in greeting.

At the farm, afternoon milking was already finished and
the Bairstow family were about to sit down at a heavy oak
table in the living-room to eat a high tea.

'What made you late?' asked Helen, two years Adrian's
elder.

16

'I missed the bus,' Adrian replied, attacking a plate of ham and salad. 'Didn't you see me waving to you to hold it up?'

'What happened?' inquired Mary Bairstow, their mother.

Adrian told them, then showed them his new purchase from Aladdin's Cave.

Always practical and forthright, Helen contended, 'I don't see any sense in buying a thing if you don't know what it is.'

'I believe I do know.'

'What is it, then?'

'I think it's a Geiger counter.'

'But if you do know, and it really is a Geiger counter, what use is it to you?'

Adrian's father, Christopher Bairstow, and his mother wisely made no comment. The drawers and cupboards in Adrian's bedroom and even shelves and nails in the farm workshop were stored with Adrian's treasures, but surprisingly he often found occasions to put his trophies to good use.

'You don't know what a Geiger counter is for,' Adrian taunted his sister.

'Of course I do, silly.'

'What is it for, then?'

'It's for counting geigers.'

Everybody laughed.

The day had been sunny and warm, but now shadows were lengthening and the evening was turning chilly. After the meal Helen went up to her study bedroom, for end-of-term examinations had not finished and she felt she must do some revision. Before going up there, however, she went to the big bookcase in the sitting-room to consult a favourite dictionary kept there. She intended to become a journalist, and she knew that journalists always have to seek correct information. Under the letter G she found what she was looking for:

GEIGER (guy'-ga) COUNTER, a cylindrical electronic device, usually held in the hand, for detecting and counting ionizing particles in order to measure radioactivity (from Hans Geiger, 1882-1945, German physicist).

☆　☆　☆

The next afternoon Adrian cycled down to the village to seek the advice of Sparky Harris. He was lucky in finding him at home, for often the doors were locked and a notice in the shop window announced 'Back Tuesday'. People in the village wondered how Sparky managed to make a living from repairing cameras and TV sets, for he often undertook jobs that could not possibly show him a profit; but he had his Naval pension and, as for closing the shop, he had many friends to visit.

'When you're out at sea for weeks at a time,' he once told Adrian, 'you need something to keep your mind interested. I get tired of novels, but I like reading technical magazines and manuals about how things work. So if it should happen that things go wrong – perhaps your radio breaks down or some bit of equipment gets lost or damaged – it's useful to know how things are put together and what to do if you have to improvise.'

Sparky was now having his afternoon tea, and at the moment Adrian arrived was eating out of a pot of home-made raspberry jam. He offered Adrian a spoonful on the same spoon. Adrian refused politely, but gracefully accepted a cup of tea. He proceeded to explain the reason for his visit and produced from his pocket the new purchase.

Sparky nodded. 'I think you're right, lad. It looks like a Geiger counter. I've never handled one before, though I've read about them.'

Adrian smiled; his hunch was proving correct.

'But you've only got part of the outfit,' Sparky

continued. 'You also need some electrical power and an amplifier and some kind of a counter.'

Adrian looked disappointed. 'But you agreed this is a counter,' he said.

'Yes, it detects radiant ions and makes a signal, but you've still got to read the signal.'

Adrian looked puzzled.

'Perhaps I'm making it difficult.' Sparky stroked the tip of his right ear while he paused to think. 'Look,' he went on, 'the Geiger counter is a kind of gas discharge tube, something like a small version of the fluorescent light that your mother has in the kitchen. So first of all you must have some electricity to energize it – to make it go. Then whenever an ion from a source of radiation passes into your Geiger counter through the window in the end' – Sparky pointed – 'it makes a slight electrical disturbance, so slight that you have to amplify it. That's what I mean by a signal. And you can pick up the signal as a click in a pair of headphones.'

Adrian's face brightened. 'I have a pair of headphones,' he said.

'Well, leave your Geiger counter with me, lad, and I'll see what I can do about the rest. If you want to make up a portable outfit you can probably get by on dry batteries, but you may have to transform some of the current into high tension. I can help you do that: there's some junk in the back of the shop that might come in useful.'

As collectors of discarded treasures, Adrian and Sparky obviously had much in common.

2

Thieves in the night

The Bairstows did not always travel to and from Westover by bus. There was the family car, used by either or both of the parents, and the children had bicycles. If there were after-school activities that did not fit in with the bus timetable, Helen and Adrian would go to school by cycle.

The shortest and easiest route for them was not the bus route, which was intended to serve the homes of the greatest number of passengers, but their own narrow lane from Up-hill Farm, south-west to meet the main road from Market Lydford to Westover, and then westward to the ancient city, an overall distance of four miles. That was the route taken by Helen on the Monday morning following Adrian's visit to Sparky Harris. Her school was preparing for a summer concert, and Helen was a highly valued member of the choir, which was to have a long rehearsal with the school orchestra late that afternoon.

She had reached the top of the hill and was free-wheeling down to the main road, when her attention was caught by a wide gap in the hedge on her left. It was not a good hedge. The meadows behind it were known as Magpie Ground, and when her father recently rented them from Colonel Savage he had had to reinforce the neglected hedge with posts and wire to make it stockproof. There was no roadside ditch on this side, only a narrow grass verge, and the road surface here was nearly on a level with the meadow beyond. Now it looked as though a heavy motor vehicle had got out of control, smashed down the posts and wire, and run on into the field.

Helen braked and jumped off her bike to investigate closer, for she knew that her father had pastured out about twenty young cattle and two or three dry cows on Magpie Ground; none of these was to be seen.

The damage looked recent, but there was no motor vehicle, only the marks of tyres, both on the verge and well into the meadow. What was more, the nature of the damage suggested to Helen that the wire might have been cut and some of the posts pulled out deliberately.

Helen decided she must tell her father as soon as possible what she had discovered. Cycling back to Up-hill Farm would make her very late for school. Remounting her bicycle, therefore, she continued down the hill to the main road and turned right for Westover. A mile along that road was a garage with petrol pumps. She feared it might not yet be open for the day, but was reassured by sight of the proprietor and lost no time in asking if she might use the telephone there.

She dialled her home number, then heard her mother's voice.

'Hello, Mummy,' she said. 'Yes, it's me. Is Daddy there?'

'No, he's somewhere about the farm.'

'Can you take a message for him? It's urgent. Something's happened.'

'Are you all right?'

'Yes. No, it's not me, it's Magpie Ground. The fence is down and all the cattle are missing. They're not in our lane, and I haven't seen any of them on the main road. I don't know what's happened to them. The fence might have been damaged accidentally by a motor, but it could have been deliberate. Daddy had better come along as soon as he can and see for himself.'

'Where are you now?'

'I'm at Peter Gurney's filling station, but I must get along

21

to school. Remember I'll be late home this evening.'

'I'll find Daddy and tell him.'

'Goodbye, then.'

Mary Bairstow was not long in finding her husband and conveying Helen's message.

'I'll go and see what's happened,' Christopher said. 'You and Danny had better stay on the farm. I hope someone will ring up to say the cattle have been found. I'll get back as soon as I can.'

He put a coil of stout wire, a bag of staples and some tools into the back of the car and drove off, up the lane and over the hill.

Catching sight of the damaged fence, Christopher approached cautiously, and parked short on the narrow verge. A quick look confirmed his worst fears. There were heavy tyre marks at all angles across the verge as though one or more vehicles had turned there, and there were tracks, where the grass was still pressed down, leading across the meadow to a belt of trees.

After a further glance at the damaged fence, Christopher followed the track marks. There were several of them, converging and diverging slightly. He noticed that in places the blades of grass were rolled down in one direction, in others the reverse. He concluded there had been two lorries, and they had been driven to the belt of trees, then back to the road.

Behind the belt of trees he found what he had half expected. The tracks stopped and the grass was heavily trampled. It was obvious that here, out of sight from any passer along the lane, the cattle had been rounded up and loaded into the lorries.

Christopher tramped around in the hope of finding further evidence or even some other explanation. He scanned the surrounding fields, vainly expecting at least to see Bluebell and the other two dry cows he had pastured here with the score of bullocks and heifers. But there was no doubt about it, the cattle had been stolen. Christopher was angry; he could hardly believe that anyone could do such a thing to him, who was always so honest with everybody.

The next thing was to get in touch with the police, so he motored down the lane and headed for Westover. Halfway along the main road he came to the filling station. He often bought petrol here, and now decided to ask the garage man if he could give any clues.

Peter Gurney, the garage man, spoke first. 'Hullo, Mr Bairstow. I saw your daughter earlier. A spot of trouble, I believe.' He would not have liked to admit that he had overheard every word and was now eager to learn of any further developments.

'It's cattle thieves, rustlers. They've stolen the cattle I had on Magpie Ground.'

'When did this happen?'

'I want to find out. Last night, I should think – or probably early this morning. Have you seen any cattle lorries about?'

'There are quite a lot of cattle lorries go past here, especially Tuesdays and Thursdays, to and from the markets.'

'What about yesterday and today?'

'I didn't open up until eight o'clock this morning, so I don't know what might have passed before that. But I didn't shut up until ten o'clock last night, and – come to think of it – yes, there were one or two cattle wagons about.'

'Which way were they going?'

'I remember now. There were two of them, coming from Westover direction. They weren't actually together: about a mile apart, one perhaps two minutes behind the other.'

'What time was it?'

'It was a light evening. About half nine, I should think; a little later perhaps. I thought they might be coming back from some gymkhana, carrying ponies or things they use for jumping.'

'Did you recognize them?'

23

'No, they weren't from round here.'

'What did they look like?'

'The first was a dull yellow colour, a sort of light brown. The second was dark blue, what you might call midnight blue.'

'Did they have any names or other lettering on them?'

'I didn't see any.'

'What about their number plates?'

'Standing here I only noticed them sideways on, and I'm afraid I didn't pay particular attention.'

Peter Gurney wore spectacles with very thick lenses. Christopher doubted if he would have been able to see much detail in the failing light.

'It sounds as though those two lorries could have been heading for Magpie Ground about nightfall.'

A fresh idea came into Christopher's head. 'Two cattle lorries from somewhere away; but somebody around here must have spied out the land. Fields right away from anywhere.'

'I sometimes feel a bit vulnerable here myself – no very near neighbours. You hear all sorts of stories about break-ins and hold-ups and muggings. But I've got my security arrangements.'

'I suppose you get all sorts calling here for petrol.'

'You can say that again. Sometimes I find them wandering round the back, probably up to no good. They always say they're looking for the toilet.'

'Have you had any strangers that look like farmers or cattle dealers or butchers?'

'Come to think of it, there's two men in a vintage car, a shiny black one. They've been past quite a number of times lately, in both directions, and they've stopped here for petrol. They're usually towing a horse trailer. The chap who drives is dark and tallish, and I've a feeling I may have met him before; probably some time ago, because I can't place him. The other is a stout man and always wears a white coat. They might be something to do with

24

racehorses; the tallish one looks a bit classy as though he might be an owner. The one in the white coat doesn't look like a butcher or a cattle dealer or even a farmer. No, he's more like a professional man slightly gone to seed – too fond of the bottle, I should think. He could be a vet, I suppose, or perhaps a steward.'

'Can you tell me anything more about them?'

'Not much. Sometimes the darkish one is driving by himself, but several times I've seen him with two workmen in blue overalls crammed into the car beside him. And once he had a different chap with him – an ugly fellow with a sort of sneer. I reckon I know him – leastways I've seen him several times at race meetings, always smoking a cigar. He's a tick-tack man. That's another reason why I connect them with racehorses.'

The conversation did not appear to be leading anywhere of practical importance, so Christopher drove on to Westover Central Police Station.

He spoke to a young uniformed constable behind the reception desk: 'I've had some cattle stolen.'

'You'd better speak to the detective sergeant; I'll see if he's free.'

The young officer spoke into his telephone.

'Yes, Detective-Sergeant Badger will see you. It's the fourth door on the right.' He pointed along a corridor, then turned to his next caller.

Christopher knocked on the door indicated, was told to enter and found himself facing a plain-clothes man seated at a desk.

'Please sit down. What can I do for you?'

Christopher came at once to the reason for his visit. 'I've had some cattle stolen.'

Detective-Sergeant Badger noted his name and address and wrote down particulars while Christopher went on to tell him of the meadows called Magpie Ground rented from Lieutenant-Colonel Savage of Walden Lodge, and how he had mended the neglected hedges with posts and wire before pasturing cattle there. His daughter had that morning found the posts and wire damaged and the cattle gone. He had at once gone to Magpie Ground to see for himself.

'Do you think your cattle could just have found a weak place and wandered out into the road?'

'No, the wire was cut and some of the posts pulled out deliberately. There were wheel marks across the verge and away into the field, and behind a spinney I found where the grass was crushed down by the wheels of two lorries and trampled by the cattle being loaded.'

The detective asked more questions. If the cattle were stolen, when did it happen? When did Christopher last see them? Could he give a more detailed description of them, and what was their value?

'Twenty young bullocks and heifers: ten of them black-and-white Hereford crosses, one light-coloured Charolais, and the rest red Devons – all beef cattle. Then there were three full-mouthed cows that had gone dry: one a blue roan, the other two black-and-white.'

'What do you mean by full-mouthed? Nothing to do with chewing the cud?'

In spite of his worry, Christopher had to smile.

'Like horses, you can tell the age of cattle and sheep by their teeth. A heifer loses her last milk teeth at about four and a half years, so at five years she has a full mouth of permanent ones; you can count eight large teeth across the front of the lower jaw.'

'I go on learning every day.'

'As to the value, that's difficult to say at this stage. You probably know the sort of price a prime beast fetches in our cattle market – several hundred pounds. Multiply that by twenty-three, and you'll have some idea of what I've lost. It's a large chunk of my livelihood.'

Detective-Sergeant Badger made careful note. 'Have you any means of identifying them?'

'They all have numbered ear tags, but that might not help. It's easy to prise a metal ear tag undone, and just as easy to put on a different tag.'

26

'Have you any idea who might have stolen your cattle?'

'Not much.' Christopher recounted in detail his conversation with Peter Gurney at the filling station.

'That sort of information might mean something or it might mean nothing,' the detective commented. 'There are lots of light-brown cattle lorries and lots of dark-blue ones; to check up on them could be like looking for a needle in a haystack. The whole operation must have been cleverly planned and timed. Your cattle will be pastured out on some remote holding by now, and the lorries will be going about their usual business today; nobody who's used to seeing them will have any idea that they've been moonlighting. But somebody must have had some inside information. Have you had anyone snooping around?'

'Not to my knowledge. Magpie Ground lies all by itself a mile away from Up-hill Farm. Anyone could pretend to take a country walk while having a good look round.'

'Have you ever found strangers along there?'

'Only two ladies with a car and a bunch of children. They were having a picnic, but they looked harmless enough.'

'What about tramps?'

'There's a derelict cottage on the corner of the lane where it meets the Market Lydford main road. I know chaps sometimes doss down there, but they're here today and gone tomorrow, and I've never had any trouble with them.'

'What about the two men with the old car, and the tick-tack man?'

'I've never seen them.'

'So, to sum up, all we've got to go on is possibly a light-brown cattle lorry and a midnight-blue one, not local, probably hunting in pairs. It doesn't sound very hopeful. I will come out to Magpie Ground and have a look for myself, and I will let you know if anything develops. I've noted your telephone number.'

'Do you mind if I leave my car on your parking space while I go along to the Farmers' Union office? I want to find

27

out how I stand on insurance.'

'That's all right. I hope you're properly covered.'

It was after lunch-time when Christopher got back to Up-hill Farm. Mary had a meal waiting for him, but he had no appetite.

3

The sale ring

The month of June seemed to pass very quickly in spite of the long days.

The school concert was a great success. Then, exams finished, Helen went with a school party for a week's course at a marine biological station on the Welsh coast.

Each evening Adrian helped his father and Danny with the hay harvest until failing light and falling dew brought the day's work to a standstill. He was especially pleased to be allowed to drive the tractor, because the previous year he had been considered too young.

'There's no need to drive fast as though you're in a motor trial,' Christopher told him. 'That's the way to make things break down. And when you're on sloping ground there are two special things to remember: don't let the tractor run away with you, and never let it tilt until it overbalances.'

Adrian had watched his father many times in the past. Now he recalled all that he had been taught and thoroughly enjoyed the experience of mechanical power under his own control.

First there was mowing. In case the weather turned wet Christopher always started his hay harvest early in June but never cut more than a few fields at a time. When sunshine had withered the mown grass it had to be turned by drawing the tedder over it, a machine armed with what

29

Helen called 'whirling spiders'. Next the dried hay had to be raked together in straight windrows. Then the tractor had to go over the ground a fourth time to pull the mechanical baler. This picked up the hay, compressed it into rectangular bales, bound them with twine and dropped them on to a tubular sledge, from which they could be released in groups at intervals by jerking a cord tied to a lever. Finally the tractor had to be driven round yet again, drawing a trailer on to which the bales were loaded and taken to a motorized elevator that carried them up and into the barn for storage.

Adrian took delight in driving as straight as the shape of each field would allow, so that he neither missed patches nor overlapped one passage with another. It was a great compliment when his father said, 'You've done that field nicely, Adrian. I couldn't have done it better myself.'

When Helen returned from Wales, she and her mother took over some of the milking and dairy work, so that Danny could take his wife, his children and his brother's family ('Denny's lot', as they were called) for a seaside holiday.

On the morning of his return to work, Danny was bursting to talk – not about his holiday but about something his brother Denny had told him. He began in the milking parlour.

'Our Denny see them wagons what take our cattle.'

Christopher's interest was at once aroused.

' 'E bin over at 'is boss's 'alf the night wi' a sow what was farrowin', an' 'e were walkin' back to 'is 'ouse just along the road, feelin' 'alf asleep I don't doubt and very pleased wi' hisself 'cause everythin' were all right. Then this gert lorry come thunderin' along behind 'e. It made 'e jump. 'E say it were one o' they gert big 'uns, an' it wad 'a' brushed 'is shoulder if 'e 'addun sidestep quick like. 'E were just recoverin' an' feelin' thankful 'e 'addun bin squash flat, when, blow me, another cattle wagon come up behind 'e just the same.'

'What time was this?'

' 'Twere Monday mornin', just after it get light, 'e say. There was one or two birds tryin' not to be the first to start singin', an' 'e notice' the rooks was peckin' up the moths what motors 'ad knock down durin' the night. 'Bout 'alf fower, mebbe.'

'And what did they look like, these cattle lorries?'

'The first were one o' they gert big 'uns, dark blue, an' it were line' out in red. Our Denny notice that, 'cause it come so close.'

'And the second?'

'All painted up smart to look like light oak; grainin' they calls it.'

'Did he see their registration numbers?'

'The first wagon go by so quick 'e diddun see, but Denny do say it weren't from round 'ere. The nex', well, 'e did see the number plate. It were FO an' some number, but 'e don't remember the figures 'cep' there was fower of them. Our Denny remember they letters, 'cause they was the same as our sister; Florence Olive she is, though we always do call 'er Flo for short.'

'Do I understand that Denny was walking back to his cottage from the farm gate, so he was on the left side of the road, with his back to Westover? Is that right?'

'Yes, that's right, Boss.'

'And the lorries were going in the same direction?'

'Yes, but o' course they was goin' quicker.'

'What I mean is that they were coming from the Westover direction, or more likely from Magpie Ground, and they were heading north.'

'That's just what I tells Denny; they was comin' from Magpie Ground, down the lane, turn right at the bottom, along the main road, and afore you gets to Westover turn right again and come upalong.'

'This is useful information. Thank your brother on my behalf. I'll pass on what he has told you to Detective-Sergeant Badger.'

'That's all right. Our mum always did say our Denny wadda made a good detective, only 'e prefer ferretin' rabbits.'

Christopher decided to telephone the Central Police Station straightaway. Detective-Sergeant Badger wasn't there, but the reception clerk took a message and the detective rang back later.

'I've got your message. I'll go and see Danny's brother myself and ask him for a statement. The registration letters FO belong to Radnorshire, but the number sounds like an old one.'

'The number plates could be false, don't you think?'

'Very likely. But they might indicate somewhere to start looking at cattle lorries. The Welsh border country is thinly populated in parts, as I expect you know. There are deep valleys and stretches of moorland with rough grazing where you will scarcely see a soul. It's quite a likely area for hiding a herd of stolen cattle.'

'Let me know if anything develops.'

'I'll keep in touch with you. Goodbye.'

☆　☆　☆

The cuckoo had already changed his tune to a stutter, when Mary Bairstow announced one morning at breakfast: 'Robin and Peg have broken up at school. They'll be here on Thursday. We'll make an early start for Westover so that I can do my week's shopping before we meet them at the coach station.'

Robin and Margaret Gaskell were her sister's children. Robin was of the same age as Adrian. Margaret was two years younger; she was always called Peg to avoid confusion with her mother, who also was named Margaret.

Helen asked, 'Will Peg be big enough to ride Pippin?'

'I expect so, but you may have to teach her.'

Pippin and Grimaldi were two ponies that Christopher Bairstow had bought as weaned foals at Market Lydford Horse Fair nearly three years before. Pippin was so called because she liked apples; her nose was particularly

32

sensitive to the faint sweetbrier scent of a ripe Cox's orange pippin. You had only to say 'Pippin' and she would come nodding her head in assent. She was a pretty bay-coloured Exmoor pony, with typical mealy muzzle and prominent wide-spaced eyes. Although she was little more than twelve hands high, her powerful loins and shoulders spoke of strength and surefootedness.

Grimaldi earned his name because he always seemed to act the clown. He was an intelligent-looking, dark-brown gelding of New Forest origin, bigger than Pippin, with rather a short neck and narrow quarters but well-set shoulders and, like Pippin, very sure feet.

It was Helen who had persuaded her father to bid for the ponies, and she had made herself responsible for managing them. Although Adrian showed an interest it was usually she who watered, fed, littered down, exercised and accustomed them to the saddle, and under her mother's guidance eventually schooled them for riding in a ring, over jumps and across country. Now they were strong four-year-olds and turned out on grass.

Thursday came, and Mary Bairstow drove into Westover with Helen and Adrian. They met the cousins at the coach station as planned, but Mary had not finished her shopping.

'You'd better take Robin and Peg down to the Market Café for a bite and a drink while I finish. I'll meet you at the car park at twelve-thirty, and we'll have a proper meal as soon as we get back to Bincombe.'

To reach the Market Café, Helen and Adrian led their cousins through the Cattle Market, where sales by auction were in progress. All four watched and listened, fascinated by the auctioneer's patter as cows were one by one brought from the pens behind, led round the sale ring and quickly sold to bidders.

Helen suddenly startled the others by crying, 'There's Bluebell! Number 125. Look!'

A blue roan cow was being led into the sale ring.

Adrian looked, and nodded in confirmation. 'What can

we do?' he asked.

Helen did not stop to give an answer. She shouted across to the auctioneer: 'That cow is stolen!'

The auctioneer was taken aback, but pretended not to hear and continued his patter.

For a moment Helen had a horrible feeling that she might be wrong, that it might be some other blue roan; but her panic quickly passed. She had fed and handled Bluebell too often to have made a mistake. She climbed over the railing in front of her, jumped down into the sale ring and ran across to the blue roan, loudly proclaiming, 'This cow is stolen!' She was sure that Bluebell now recognized her too.

There was a murmur among the farmers and dealers crowded round the ring.

The auctioneer could no longer ignore the interruption. 'We will put number 125 back,' he announced briskly. 'Now, number 126: what am I bid for number 126?'

Bluebell was led out of the ring, closely followed by Helen, who was turning over in her mind what to do next. Adrian pushed his way through the farmers and dealers, to join her.

'Adrian, find the nearest policeman. Send him to me here, then go on to the Central Police Station and see if you can speak to Detective-Sergeant Badger.'

It was well after twelve-thirty when Helen, Adrian, Robin and Peg rejoined Mary at the car park. They all tried to speak at once, and she could scarcely make herself heard, to say, 'We'd better telephone Father.'

'It's all done,' Adrian told her gleefully. 'He's waiting at home for you to bring the car back so that he can come down to Westover and claim Bluebell himself.'

Helen added, 'Sergeant Badger says that, if the Superintendent of Police can get a magistrate to make a possession order, Bluebell might be home before dark. Otherwise she may have to be impounded until the next sessions. So let's get moving. We're all famished.'

Peg started to giggle.

34

'What is it, Peg?'

'Just think of Bluebell appearing in court. She would look splendid in the witness box!'

4

Golden saxifrage

Robin and Peg were quickly made to feel at home at Up-hill Farm. Pippin was just the right size for Peg, who had done a little riding already and had brought a riding hat in her luggage. In the days that followed she proved to be an apt pupil for Helen. As for Robin, he was pleased but not wildly excited at the prospect of spending a few weeks on the farm and going fishing with Adrian.

Peg was especially charmed by Esmeralda, the farm cat, a smooth-haired tortoiseshell with gooseberry-green eyes. At the time of the cousins' arrival Esmeralda was expecting her first litter of kittens. Recently she had paid repeated visits to the loft over the stable, not her usual haunt. Mary thought this was significant and might indicate the event was soon to happen, for the loft was dry and warm, with soft sacks and loose hay scattered about and little risk of disturbance from humans or other animals.

Like most of the farm buildings, the stable was built of local stone and roofed with pantiles. A stone staircase ran up the gable end to give access to the loft; and Peg, who was fascinated by plants as well as animals, noticed that its joints provided root-holds for hart's-tongue ferns wherever rain water trickled down, and for little rusty-back ferns in other places; these were rarities in the drier part of the country where her home was.

Up-hill Farm lay above the village of Bincombe on the

Walden Hills, a twenty-mile chain of flat-topped limestone hillocks rising to a thousand feet. When the Romans came to Britain they discovered ores of lead and silver in these hills, and they made straight roads for communication with their colonies and for sending ingots of metal away by pack animals. Their roads can still be traced on maps, but although some of them have become motor highways, others or parts of them have fallen into disuse and are now no more than cart tracks and bridle paths. There were plenty of these around Bincombe, and they made ideal rides for Helen and Peg: there was no motor traffic, and the soft turf that carpeted them removed any risk of hammering their ponies' joints, as could happen when cantering on hard roads.

Earlier colonists, Bronze Age and Iron Age people, also left tracks from one hill-top site to another, sometimes leading straight up and down but often winding to ease gradients. The sides of the hills are still partly wooded, but the hill tops and the lower ground along their flanks have long since been cleared for grazing.

The Bairstows owned their farm, but much of the adjoining land, nearly five thousand acres of woodland and rough pasture, formed the Walden Lodge estate of the Savage family. Lieutenant-Colonel John Henry Irving Savage, DSO, the present owner, had had a successful Army career, then became a world traveller and explorer. Now over seventy years of age, he lived a frugal bachelor life at Walden Lodge, looked after by two old servants.

'Things were very different at Walden Lodge once upon a time,' Christopher Bairstow told the children at supper one evening. 'I can remember when I was a boy the stable block up there used to house polo ponies, hunters and a shining carriage and pair. As you know, I rent Magpie Ground from the Colonel, and instead of posting him a cheque I go up to Walden Lodge around quarter day, to pay him the rent in person. He likes a chat, and I know he's always glad of the money. Last time I was up there I found him in the coach-house. All he's got in there now is a little old mini-car, a three-speed bicycle and a worm-eaten wheelbarrow.'

Relaxed by his meal, Christopher pushed back his chair and went on talking.

'The Colonel won't mind if you ride on his estate, provided you don't do any damage. He likes children, though he's never had any of his own. Only a good-for-nothing step-nephew, his late sister's stepson, Gerontius d'Arcy.

'I feel rather sorry for the old chap. He was very wealthy once. That was how he was able to travel so widely. But he put this so-called nephew to manage his estate and look after his business affairs while he was away, and when he came back from his travels he found he was ruined. While the Colonel was away the nephew sold the Colonel's stocks and shares, which were previously in good companies, then gambled the money on the Stock Exchange by reinvesting in whatever promised higher dividends or quick profits. He didn't stop at that either, but put money into some shady enterprises with no proper security.'

'But the Colonel still owns this big estate, doesn't he?' Helen asked. 'That ought to bring him in a good income.'

'It's mostly what is called marginal land. There are only a few smallholdings to bring him in rent, and they all need capital investment. After he returned from abroad the Colonel was full of enthusiasm to improve farm buildings and houses on his estate, but when he came to realize some of his investments he found they'd already been sold, and when he pressed his nephew for the money he found it had been squandered. I don't think he would have taken legal action against his own sister's stepson, but other people had been cheated as well, and they complained to the authorities until there was a criminal prosecution. Gerry d'Arcy was given a gaol sentence for embezzlement.

'Anyway, carry on taking the ponies up the hill and have some good rides.'

Christopher rose from the table, and the others followed

his example.

It was next day that Helen decided to take Peg down to Magpie Ground.

Christopher had not yet mended the fence there; although time was passing he was reluctant to alter anything that might still yield evidence of the cattle theft. As to the future, he could ill afford to buy more store cattle to replace those stolen, and until the affair was cleared up he did not wish to take the risk of having yet more cattle stolen. He had concluded that his best plan for Magpie Ground would be to let the grass grow, then mow it – for use as hay where it was good enough, or for bedding where the quality was poor.

Bluebell was home again, but there was no news of the other cattle. Detective-Sergeant Badger was hopeful that tracing Bluebell's travels might reveal what had happened to the other two dry cows. All three had obviously passed through several dealers' hands, he said, and that was how Bluebell had unwittingly been brought back to home territory after being taken perhaps a hundred miles away.

'Dealers are honest fellows mostly,' he said, 'but they don't like talking about their business or their clients to a policeman. If he is in plain clothes they can usually still tell and are even more on their guard.'

Peg's lessons on Pippin had so far been conducted mostly around the farm yard and in Five-acre, where Peg had become used to trotting and was learning how to put the pony into a canter.

'Let's have a change today,' said Helen. 'We'll go up the lane and over the hill.'

This they did.

'Daddy says we must be careful not to obliterate any evidence,' Helen told Peg as they approached Magpie Ground. 'Detective-Sergeant Badger has been out to see for himself; he has taken photos of wheel tracks and had some plaster casts made of tyre prints. I don't think he's the sort of man to leave any stone unturned, but Daddy

39

still hopes he might send out a forensic scientist who might discover something more. I wish we could help.'

Helen and Peg halted their ponies while they looked at the damaged fencing.

'We may as well go down to the bottom of the lane,' Helen suggested. 'There's nothing special down there, only a derelict cottage on the corner.'

They walked the ponies on. When they reached the main road and were about to turn back, Peg said she would like to look inside the cottage. It would be a useful exercise for Peg to dismount and find a way of hitching her pony securely, so Helen let her do so and did the same herself.

The cottage gate was broken and hanging on only one hinge. They picked their way over broken roof tiles and rank weeds to the front door, which was jammed half open. They went in.

'This place hasn't been lived in as long as I can remember,' Helen told Peg. 'I think it must have been built here for a shepherd or a gamekeeper. I can't imagine any woman ever wanting to live here all alone and without any mod. cons.'

'Is there a ghost, do you think?'

Helen didn't like anything spooky, so she said, 'I most certainly don't think.'

As if to contradict her a rusty hinge creaked upstairs. Helen said, 'That's only the wind.'

In the single downstair living-room and the lean-to leading from it they found no more than Helen had expected: fallen plaster, cobwebs, a smell and feeling of dampness, a few worm-eaten remnants of furniture. The rusty grate was choked with ashes and soot. Hearth and window-sills were cluttered with empty beer-bottles. Upstairs (and Helen warned Peg to tread carefully in case any stairs or floorboards were rotten) things were little different – worse, in fact, for a large area of ceiling had fallen, revealing rotted joists and rafters, and beyond them a patch of blue sky where roof tiles were missing.

Remembering the ponies tethered outside, the girls did not stay long. If Helen had secretly hoped they might find something that would give a clue to the cattle robbery, she was disappointed. It was pleasant to come out into the warm sunshine, remount the ponies and make their way back up the lane.

On Helen's instruction they rode in single file on the right-hand side, Peg in front, where Helen could keep her under observation. As they came to the place where the fencing was damaged, Peg drew rein. She looked down at the ditch that ran along the opposite side of the lane.

'What is it, Peg?'

'Do you know you've got some golden saxifrage growing along this ditch?'

'No, I didn't. Have you spotted some?'

'You could find two sorts, with different leaves and different stems. I'd like to see which sort this is.'

Helen held Pippin's bridle while Peg dismounted; it was good practice for her. Helen did not wish to appear uninterested in wild flowers when Peg was obviously keen, so she said, 'Is that tall plant in the ditch the greater willow-herb? We call it "codlins and cream".'

Peg was already scrambling down the bank. The ponies caught the scent of crushed meadowsweet and water mint; they edged nearer. The bottom of the ditch was full of water, moving slowly through a jungle of marsh plants.

Reaching over to pick a sprig of golden saxifrage, Peg lost her balance, slipped, and found herself clinging to the tall stems of willow-herb for support. She was wearing shoes, not wellington boots, and her feet were in nine inches of water.

'That's funny,' she said. 'I felt something hard.'

'I'm glad you find it funny. You won't mind if I laugh.'

'Something pressed against my ankle.'

Without wasting words, Peg made herself still wetter by foraging among the water weeds.

'I've got it!' she cried, and pulled up a dark strip of metal.

41

'It's an old number plate.' She held it up for Helen to see. 'A front one, I should think, because there are only two holes for fixing; none for a rear light. It says FO 1185. I wonder who lost that.'

'FO something, did you say? Oh, Peg, it's the sort of clue I've been praying for. It could have fallen off one of the cattle lorries as it was turning out of Magpie Ground.'

Peg's interest in golden saxifrage momentarily dwindled in the excitement of finding what might be a vital clue for Uncle Chris. She climbed up the bank, pulled off her shoes and socks, and did a little dance on the grass before shaking out the water and putting them on again.

The girls remounted the ponies and made their way back to Up-hill Farm. Helen carried the number plate as far as the farm gate; then, wet as she still was and despite the necessity of keeping a correct seat and holding the reins properly, Peg was allowed to enter the yard triumphantly displaying her new-found registration number.

Christopher caught sight of her, and his air of gloom changed. 'Three Oscars for Peg!' he cried, as soon as he had heard her story. 'I'll ring up Detective-Sergeant Badger straightaway. Now he can have something definite to work on.'

5

Trouble at the Pool

It was Saturday morning. At breakfast Christopher announced that Esmeralda had had her kittens.

'How many?' Helen asked.

'I counted four.'

'What colour are they?' Peg wanted to know.

'So far as I could see there were an all-black one, a tortoiseshell, a tabby and a ginger.'

Mary said, 'I expect Doctor Hobday's black pussy, Anthracite, has had something to do with this.'

Robin gave a hesitant cough, which Peg recognized as a sign he was trying to make a joke. 'Do you mean that Esmeralda has been going to the Doctor's?' he asked.

Mary smiled. 'You could put it like that,' she agreed.

In spite of good appetites, nobody spent long in finishing the meal, and the four cousins trooped up the stone steps at the end of the stable to admire Esmeralda's offspring.

'What are you two boys planning to do today?' Mary inquired when they returned.

'I've bought a trout licence for Robin,' Adrian replied, 'so now I can take him down to the Pool. I've got a spare rod for him.'

Walking down the lane from Up-hill Farm to the village, Adrian told his cousin that Bincombe Pool belonged to the Parish Council but a number of local residents had formed an angling club to lease it.

'We restock it every springtime with brown trout, and they grow very well because there's plenty of natural food for them – shrimps and insect larvae and that sort of thing. Rainbow trout might grow faster, but we can't keep them in. We tried rainbows once, but they all made off downstream. I'm a club member, and any member is allowed to catch one brace of trout per day. I don't know why we always say "brace"; it only means two. A member may bring a visitor to fish, but they mustn't take away more than two fish between them.'

The Pool lay on the lower side of the village, fed by the Bin Brook. There were Norman columns in Bincombe Parish Church, and tradition had it that Norman monks not only built the church but built the stone dam across the brook to make a fish pond.

'Part of the fun of trout fishing is stalking your fish,' Adrian explained as they approached the water's edge. 'It may give its position away by breaking surface to catch a fly. Then you tempt it by dropping an artificial fly in front of its nose. Of course the artificial fly hides a small hook attached to your line. If the fish takes your lure it will try to get away and you'll have to tire it out by playing it. When you can slip a landing net under it and bring it to the bank without damage, I can promise you, no fish has ever tasted better than a nicely cooked trout you have caught yourself.'

Robin thought Adrian sounded a little conceited, but he listened attentively. 'There are some flies dancing up and down over the water now,' he observed.

'Those are mayflies,' Adrian told him. 'If you could catch one you would probably find it has two pairs of wings – that is to say two large fore wings and two small hind wings – and three tails. Look, there's a spent fly floating on the surface; I'll pick it up on the handle of my landing net.'

He did so, and they both peered at the exhausted insect.

'This is the sort of mayfly we call a pond olive. It's interesting because it's a kind in which the hind wings no

44

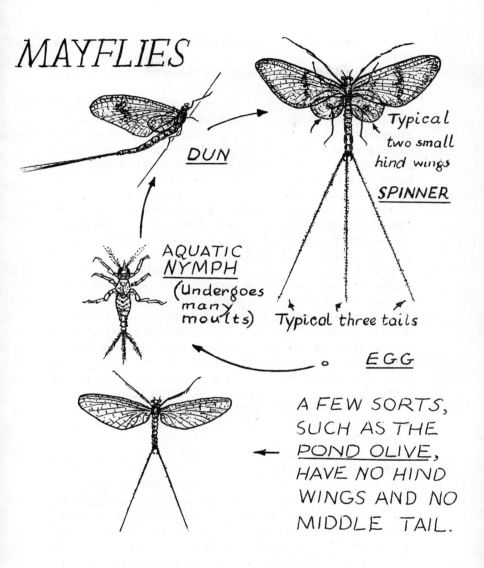

MAYFLIES

DUN

Typical
two small
hind wings

SPINNER

AQUATIC
NYMPH
(Undergoes
many
moults)

Typical three tails

∘ *EGG*

A FEW SORTS,
SUCH AS THE
POND OLIVE,
HAVE NO HIND
WINGS AND NO
MIDDLE TAIL.

This is a drawing that Adrian made for Robin, to illustrate
what he had told him about mayflies.

45

longer develop, and actually there is no middle tail either.'

'But you said they are mayflies, and that mayflies have two pairs of wings and three tails.'

'I said "probably", because as a rule mayflies do have two pairs of wings and three tails; but this is one of the exceptions. However, I don't suppose a trout stops to count either wings or tails.' Adrian pulled a flat tin box from a pocket. 'I've got one or two imitation pond olives here. They are made of feather, fine wire and coloured silk thread. Let's try one.'

He put a rod and reel together, threaded a line and showed Robin how to cast an artificial fly. Leaving Robin to practise casting, he put a rod together for himself. Soon both boys were searching the Pool for fish and casting their lures over them.

The day passed very pleasantly, and later when they presented Mary Bairstow with a brace of trout for the table there was great jubilation that one of them had been caught and landed by Robin. His holiday, he reflected, was not working out too badly. He was pleased when Adrian took considerable trouble to make a drawing of mayflies for him, to illustrate what he had been talking about that morning.

Two days later they went fishing again. Robin nearly hooked a fish but lost it; Adrian again caught and landed a sizeable trout.

They walked up the hill to the farm at midday for some lunch, then back to the Pool early in the afternoon. The morning had been dull, with occasional bursts of sunshine, but by afternoon the clouds were few, the sun blazed down and mayflies were emerging from the water surface. Adrian called Robin's attention to the way in which this happened. He was lucky in finding a mayfly nymph creeping up a water plantain; they watched it spread its new-found wings and inflate its body into a dull-looking and not very attractive winged insect.

'That's called a dun,' Adrian said; 'but just wait and

46

see.'

They had to wait several minutes. The sun warmed the dun and dried it. Then they saw it stretch out its wings, its outer skin split down the back and a shining perfect mayfly wriggled out. It paused for a moment before flitting upward to join the swarm of similar mayflies that rose and fell over the water.

'That's what is called a spinner,' Adrian stated, 'the adult mayfly.'

They resumed their fishing, but although it was pleasant to be by the waterside they had no further success.

'I guess the trout have got fed up with pond olives,' Adrian concluded. 'They've had enough. We can try something different, but fish do get sated when there's a really good hatch, and in hot weather they can go right off their food, whatever is offered.'

They tried other flies from the tin box, but to no avail.

'Would it be better early in the morning?' Robin suggested.

'Yes, or in the cool of the evening.'

'Let's come down early tomorrow, say before breakfast.'

So it was arranged: next day the boys had an early-morning cup of tea with Christopher, then walked down to Bincombe Pool while he went to join Danny in the milking parlour.

The church clock struck the quarter-hour after six, and Robin instinctively looked at his watch. It was a new wrist-watch with all the features he had wanted, for it was stainless and waterproof and self-winding, and had a date window and luminous hands and figures. He had put together all the money presents he had received on his last birthday, and his parents had made up the rest of the cost. Peg was a little envious but had been told she must start saving and do the same as Robin when her next birthday came round.

There was very little traffic moving in Bincombe at that

hour. As Adrian and Robin crossed the High Street they saw a red van arrive at the Post Office Stores, but otherwise all was quiet. As they approached the Pool, however, they became aware of a commotion.

A flock of coots at the Pool's margin ran along the water surface, splashing vigorously before rising clear, wings beating rapidly, only to come down at the far end of the Pool, alighting with more splashes, breast forward, feet lowered. A family of young mallards broke cover from alders on the bank, springing clear of the water, shooting upward and flying round in a circle before they too in their own manner came down near the lower end of the Pool, feet forward, their tails ploughing quite a wash.

The reason for the birds' flight was not at first apparent, but then the boys noticed that something unusual was happening at the top end of the Pool where the brook issued from a stone culvert. Large numbers of trout and minnows were displaying strange activity, swimming fast, shooting out of the water as if trying to escape from something, skittering in the surface, then suddenly going limp and apparently lifeless. The boys watched as a huge trout shot up from deep down with a powerful swirl of its body and seemed to fly through the air before hitting the surface of the water and rolling drunkenly on its side.

'I didn't know we had any fish as big as that, nor so many little ones,' Adrian declared. 'Really, this is most unusual. Something must have happened.'

They observed a greyish cloud creeping through the Pool from the top end. It moved slowly, but as it progressed it spread wider, and wherever it spread it intensified the activity of any animal life there. Freshwater shrimps leaped from under the surface; waterboatmen uttered shrill whistles and rowed as if for a boat race; whirligig beetles rotated like spinning tops.

'I wonder if something has been washed into the brook higher up. Perhaps workmen have been flushing the water main,' Adrian speculated.

'Would they have started work so early?'

'It's quite possible. The brook starts somewhere up the hill. Then there's another stream comes in from our farm on the other side of the lane. I don't believe our Dad would let any sheep dip or silage liquor get into it but I'll ask him if he's done anything unusual. Silage liquor is brown, anyway, not greyish, and we haven't made silage this year, the weather's been so good for making hay. The only other farm is Binbrook Farm, and that's over there, downstream of the Pool.'

The boys tried to resume their fishing, but it was no good. Reluctantly they packed up their tackle.

'Shouldn't we take a sample of the water?' Robin asked.

'What in?'

They looked around, but visitors to the Pool were requested to be tidy, and not a discarded bottle or beer can was to be seen.

'I know,' said Adrian at last; 'a gumboot.'

The cloudy water was becoming diluted as it moved downstream; the greatest concentration was close to the stone culvert. Before taking off one of his wellington boots, Adrian tried reaching out over the brook, but the bank here was steep and offered no foothold and he could not reach far enough for a sample of the greyish cloud.

'It's no good trying here; we'll have to go further along where the shore is flatter.'

'Isn't that a boat over on the other side?' Robin asked. 'We could use that to get right up to the culvert, where the cloudiness is greatest.'

'A good idea.'

They picked up their tackle and ran round to the other side of the Pool. There on the bank lay a little boat, a pram dinghy that might once have been the tender for a small yacht. A pair of oars and two rowlocks lay in the bottom. A long chain was wound round the seat amidship, its free end padlocked to a ring-bolt on a stout post set in the bank.

Adrian tried the padlock, but it was shut tight: the ring

and the post too were quite immovable. Robin examined the other end of the chain and found it was secured by a shackle under the seat. The pin of the shackle was screwed in hard, but Adrian produced his pocket knife with a spike in the handle, and in less than a minute the pin was undone, the chain was unwound and the boat was slid down the bank and on to the water.

Both boys scrambled into the boat, Adrian pushing off from the land as he did so. But even before Robin could fit the rowlocks into place it was apparent that something had been overlooked, for water was flooding into the boat from a round hole in the bottom. They quickly searched the boat for the plug that fitted the hole, but nothing suitable was found. Robin dropped the oars into the rowlocks and tried to row back to land, but water had risen above their ankles before they grounded on the shore.

Adrian leapt out and searched the mooring place for a cork or any other kind of bung, but without success. Robin meanwhile tried to plug the hole with his handkerchief, but it was not until he hit on the idea of folding his handkerchief and rolling it round a stub of pencil that he achieved anything like the right shape, and he had to unroll and refold the hanky differently several times before he obtained the right thickness.

Adrian took off one of his wellingtons to use as a baler. He pushed off again. Robin's plug seemed to be holding in place even if not absolutely watertight. 'We're all right now,' Adrian said.

Robin burst into song, 'Come, cheer up, mi lads, 'tis to glory we steer,' and he pulled on the oars, sending the dinghy briskly up to the head of the Pool.

'You can lay on your sculls now, my hearty,' Adrian told him, trying to match Robin's nautical mood. Now he leaned over the stern and tried to dip his wellington boot into the water, but it tended to float and he had to shift his position to push it under just where he wanted; then, when the boot was full of cloudy water, its weight pulled him down and he had to move again to exert sufficient lift to bring it inboard over the side. The combined result of such movements in so small a boat was nearly a capsize, but Robin countered by letting go of his oars and moving his weight to the opposite side. He should have foreseen that one of the oars would slide out of its rowlock and start drifting away.

Some of the precious water sample had been spilt by the rocking of the boat, but Robin now kept the wellington boot upright while Adrian grabbed the remaining oar, and standing in the stern sculled after its fellow.

It was only when he reached it, and Robin had restored both oars to their rowlocks and started pulling for the post on the shore, that Adrian had an afterthought.

'I ought to have washed that boot out thoroughly before filling it with the water sample,' he reflected.

'But you slopped a lot of water into and out of it when you were baling with it.'

'That wasn't clean water, and I didn't use my hand to swish it round down at the foot. I'd better get another sample.'

Reluctantly Robin rowed back to the head of the Pool; but the cloudiness there was already beginning to diminish.

'We'd better keep the first sample, but I'll fill my other boot as well,' Adrian decided, and he pulled off his other wellington, washed it out thoroughly, flung the washings away on the far side of the boat and filled it as best he could from the waning cloud.

This time the sampling was accomplished without mishap. Robin rowed back to the mooring post; the boots full of cloudy water were lifted out of the boat carefully; both boys heaved the dinghy up the bank; Robin retrieved his handkerchief and stub of pencil, and the chain and shackle were reinstated as they were found.

The boys made their way slowly, Adrian barefooted, through Bincombe and up the lane towards Up-hill Farm. Before reaching this, however, they came to a stone building nearly opposite the farm house. Its windows were protected by wire screens and it stood in a grassy enclosure surrounded by iron railings. On the downhill side could be seen a marshy patch and a stream of water welling up from under a rock.

'That's where the Bin Brook starts,' Adrian told his cousin. 'You know, the one that feeds the Pool. We might have a look around here after breakfast.'

'Don't you think we ought to do it now, while the trail is fresh?'

'Oh, all right.' Adrian put down the boot he was carrying, and Robin did the same. 'This place is called the Meter House, so I suppose it houses a big meter on the water main, though I've never been inside to see. It's kept locked up.'

From where they were standing the water in the brook looked clear and colourless, but to get a closer look Adrian saved his bare feet from stinging nettles by clambering along the iron railings before sliding down the bank.

Robin pushed open the gate of the enclosure and walked across to watch Adrian paddling in the brook. He called attention to a stout iron pipe discharging just below him. Adrian bent down to sniff the mouth of the pipe and let the jet play on his hands before confirming that it was only clean water.

'What are the splashes of white on those big stones in the brook?' Robin asked.

'Oh, nothing much. Bird droppings. Dippers. You sometimes see one bobbing up and down at the water's edge. They can actually walk on the bed of the stream under water, hunting for food; they use their wings like fins to keep themselves down. They are very shy, so I don't suppose we shall see one while we're here, though one could be watching us all the time.'

Adrian followed the brook downstream until it passed into a thicket. Retracing his steps carefully, for there were potholes and slabs of rock slippery with silkweed, he found a crayfish caught up in water moss. He disentangled it gingerly, half-expecting to be nipped; but the crayfish was dead. He threw it up to Robin, who let it fall on the grass before picking it up suspiciously and sniffing at it.

'It doesn't stink,' Robin said.

'It must be fresh, then; not long dead.'

'That might be significant. But one swallow does not make a summer. Are there any more?'

Adrian looked carefully, but there were no more crayfish, dead or alive. He climbed back along the railings and joined Robin, who had flung the crayfish away and was trying the handle of the Meter House door – but to no avail, for the heavy door was securely locked. They circled the building, but undisturbed grass and moss in the joints of cover plates only suggested that no workmen had been busy there.

Reluctantly the boys closed the gates behind them, picked up the wellington boots and made their way across the lane to Up-hill Farm and a belated breakfast.

6

Danny runs amuck

Christopher Bairstow was later than usual coming in for breakfast.

'I don't know what's the matter with Danny,' he said. 'It's not only shirt buttons. He's gone right off his rocker.'

Danny's sinewy arms and long legs ended in hands and feet seemingly large as shovels. Birds might have mistaken him for a scarecrow. His round blue eyes and big nose were set in a weather-beaten face crowned by a mop of wavy black hair tousled by the wind. His clothes looked as though they had fallen on him rather than been put on and might fall off again, and his open-necked shirt inevitably had the buttons at variance with the buttonholes. Nevertheless he was a likeable fellow and a good farm worker who could turn his hand to anything from building a dry stone wall to lambing an exhausted ewe.

'What's the trouble?' asked Mary.

'When I joined him this morning he was in the milking parlour singing "Wraggle-taggle gipsies, O" at the top of his voice.'

'There's nothing wrong in that, is there?'

'No, but he was beating time by working a cow's tail up and down like a pump handle.'

'Then what happened?'

'I told him to get on with his work properly, which he did for a time.'

'Was he all right after that?'

'Not exactly. A short while later I went into the dairy, and when I came back into the milking parlour Danny wasn't there. I called his name but he didn't answer. Then I looked outside, where the cows were going back to the fields, and there was Danny riding on the back of Daisy, holding on to her horns. He was singing, "O saddle for me my milk-white steed"; but it didn't last long, because next he tried to stand up on Daisy's haunches like a circus ballerina. He'd just reached "What care I for a goose-feather bed?" when Daisy shot him off on to the muck heap.'

'He must have been drunk,' Mary suggested.

'He didn't try to get up, just lay there as if in a dream.'

'Do you think he was hurt?'

'I asked him if he felt all right, but he was so confused I couldn't get any sense out of him except that he wasn't really hurt. He looked very pale – pale for him, that is – so I told him to go home until he felt better. He rolled rather than walked. I think he must have been on the bottle. But it's not like Danny; he's supposed to be a regular temperance man.'

'Did he smell?' asked Helen.

'I bet he did after he fell in the muck heap,' giggled Peg, who had been listening wide-eyed.

'I mean, did his breath smell?'

'No worse than usual.'

'Did it smell of alcohol?' Helen persisted.

'I can't say that it did.'

'Perhaps he's had a drop of cider,' Mary suggested, 'and not being used to it, it's gone to his head.'

It was at this point that Adrian and Robin came in for breakfast. They were hungry and bursting to tell what had been happening down at the Pool. Adrian paid little attention to the story of Danny's strange behaviour; but Robin, who could never resist a pun, however horrible, coughed discreetly before remarking, 'Now I know how anyone runs *amuck.*'

Breakfast over, Adrian made for the farmhouse pantry, picked out the two largest of the empty bottles there, washed them and their stoppers until there was no longer a smell of vinegar, and took them out to the back door, where he and Robin had left the wellington boots full of water. One boy holding a bottle, the other gently tilting a floppy boot, they filled first one bottle from one boot, then the second bottle from the other. The water didn't appear so cloudy when held up to the light, and there was little apparent difference between the first bottle and the second, but they both looked like dirty water rather than clean tap water.

Robin screwed on the stoppers while Adrian went to look for some gummed labels.

'What shall I write?' he asked when he returned.

'What it is, where it is from, day and time,' Robin suggested.

Then the question arose, which bottleful was the first sample taken; but having agreed that it was his left wellington he had filled first, Adrian wrote: 'Sample 1. Cloudy water from Bincombe Pool, Tuesday, 7.25 a.m.' While Robin stuck the label on the still-wet side of the first bottle, Adrian wrote again: 'Sample 2. Cloudy water from Bincombe Pool, Tuesday, 7.30 a.m.'

They stood the bottles in a corner of the pantry. Adrian washed out his wellingtons and left them upside down under the back porch to drain and dry.

7

'Sort of pixillated'

Something unusual was happening among the inhabitants of Bincombe.

Doctor Richard Hobday was senior partner in a medical practice at Westover known as Drs Hobday, McBrayne & Williams, but he lived at Bincombe and held a surgery there from eight-thirty to ten o'clock on Tuesday and Friday mornings. Unlike the Westover clinic, this was conducted casually, with no receptionist or timed appointments.

This Tuesday the Doctor's first patient was Miss Alfreda Jones, the sister of the Bincombe Sub-Postmaster. She was a middle-aged spinster, always business-like and civil to customers at the Post Office, who nevertheless found her aloof, impersonal and scarcely the sort of person to crack a joke with. This morning, however, when Alfreda came into the consulting-room she flung her arms around Doctor Hobday and kissed him warmly on both cheeks.

'*Dear* Doctor Hobday! *Reelly*, I am so glad to see you,' she declared.

'Thank you for the compliment, Miss Jones. What brings you here this morning?'

'Doctor, I've come over all funny. It's only since I got up. *Atchully*, I'm sort of pixillated.'

'What do you mean by pixillated?'

'I feel as if I'm floating. Look, Doctor, I'll tell you how it happened. I mean, I always have two big cups of tea to wake me up properly before the early mail van calls. I call them *les tasses du jour,* and I like to sit quiet and comfortable for a little, while I drink them. One cup is never enough to wake me up properly. Atchully, this morning, just as the mail van arrived, I could feel myself coming over all funny. Reelly, for a moment I believed I was a fleecy cloud in the sky. Dreamy, you know, as if nothing mattered. I mean, the postman just stood there with the mail bags, looking at me, but reelly I couldn't make the effort to take them or to give him the packets from yesterday afternoon. And yet atchully I felt excited, as if something lovely was going to happen. And I still do, Doctor. My brother said I'd better come over and see you. "Elfie," he said (he always calls me Elfie, and so do my friends – my best friends, that is, not just ordinary people like you get in the Post Office), "Elfie," he said, "you'd better go over to Beech House and see that nice Doctor Hobday." So I've come over to see you.'

She certainly seemed unusually excited. The Doctor asked questions, felt her pulse, took her temperature, sounded her heart with his stethoscope and measured her blood pressure with his manometer. When he looked into her eyes she again tried to embrace him. This morning she was nothing like the demure Miss Alfreda Jones who sold him stamps over the Post Office counter.

At last, 'I don't think there is very much wrong with you, Miss Jones,' he said, 'certainly nothing you need worry about. We all feel a bit unusual at times.'

At that moment he himself felt 'a bit unusual' but could not explain it or indeed Alfreda Jones's condition. He thought for a while.

'I won't give you a prescription now,' he said. 'But I would like you to go home and lie down, sleep if you can. If you feel better you can carry on with your work. I would like you to come here again on Friday morning. If you feel any worse in the meantime you can ring me up or get someone to do so for you.'

He dared not get up to open the door for her in case she made another boisterous assault upon him. Instead he said, 'Will you ask the next patient to come in, please?'

The next patient was shouting but quietened down in the consulting-room when the Doctor shut the door. He was a retired road worker named Charles Barlow, but everyone called him Charley Barley.

'I were a-comin' to see you about me arthuritis,' he began at once. 'It's bin very bad lately, terrible painful. But this mornin', after I have me three cupsa tea, it's all gone, so I keeps askin' meself what I'm a-doin' wastin' me time comin' yer like.'

The Doctor asked him a few questions, then said: 'So you're all right now. I shan't need to see you again until winter strikes once more.'

Charley went out, but the waiting-room was still crowded and noisy. One by one the Doctor admitted his patients to the consulting-room, questioned and examined them, and sometimes prescribed a remedy. At last he picked up the telephone and dialled his health clinic at Westover.

'Hello, there. This is Richard Hobday speaking from Beech House. Put me through to Doctor McBrayne, please.'

There was a pause, then: 'Hello, Ian. I say, I've something like an epidemic on my hands this morning. All the village . . . well, perhaps one in twenty. . . .

'Signs and symptoms? To put it briefly, they've all gone mad. Hallucinations, *joie de vivre,* morbid tears. You should have seen Alfreda Jones kissing me on both cheeks . . . Yes, the prissy one. . . .

'Seriously, though, they all have various degrees of exhilaration. Some felt dizzy, others just dreamy. . . . Slow pulse; breathing rather slow and laboured; faces pale, not florid. Eyes, oh yes, contracted pupils, typical pin-points – that's one reason I rule out alcohol. Really, you'd think they'd all been smoking opium, chasing the dragon. But that's impossible, so it must be something else. . . .

'They all say it came on suddenly about breakfast-time this morning. . . . Yes, all of them. . . . Food poisoning? I doubt it. There's no stomach cramp, no sickness; some a little loose in the bowels, perhaps. . . . No fever, no sore throats. . . .

'Yes, one or two said they had vague headaches; some said itching, others sweating. Come to think of it, I feel a bit strange myself. . . . No, it's not a hangover. . . .

'Have you any similar cases? . . . Not yet. Well, let me know if you do, and please ask Doctor Williams to do the same. It could be an infection, but a strange one; some new virus, perhaps. . . . Yes, I've taken some swabs and I'm sending them to the P.H. Lab. direct. We'll just have to await developments.'

A little later, refreshed by a cup of coffee but still feeling 'a bit unusual' if not actually unsure of his movements, Doctor Hobday started out on his round of visits. As he drove his silver-grey car out of the village he was surprised to see the cattle at Binbrook Farm, tails horizontal, chasing round the field as if in a steeplechase.

'They must be sort of pixillated,' he murmured.

He stopped the car and looked at his eyes, one at a time, in the driving mirror.

'*Atchully,*' he told himself, 'I'm a bit pixillated myself.'

8

Radioactivity

With Danny off work, Helen volunteered to take over whatever had to be done in the dairy for the rest of the morning. She had intended to take Peg for a ride up the combe and possibly up to Bradbury Castle, but after some discussion with her parents she agreed that Peg was now experienced enough to ride by herself. Helen helped her saddle up Pippin and gave directions.

'You go up our lane about half a mile, and at the top of the rise there's a green track that cuts across it. You turn left along the green track. After another half-mile you will find the track forks. The left-hand fork is just a bridle path, and if you follow it you will find it takes you right up to Bradbury Castle. It's not actually a castle with battlements and that sort of thing, just an Iron Age camp on the top of a hill, and it's quite flat on top. You can go up there on Pippin and ride all the way round the embankment and come down again. The other fork at the bottom goes on for a long way, but a short distance along is an old quarry on your left enclosed in a wire fence with a five-barred gate. You will know when you get there because there's a notice that says "Caution. Falling rocks". That's the way into the Treacle Mine.'

'The Treacle Mine?' Peg repeated incredulously. 'You don't get treacle from a mine.'

'Oh, that's just a joke. Everybody in our village calls it that. It's supposed to have been a Roman lead mine, but it

61

was worked again in the eighteenth century, so there are passages running all over the place inside the hill and cutting into the natural caves. I've never been in there because it's been shut up as long as I can remember, but Father says that right in the heart of the hill is a stupendous cave called the Roman Cavern with a lake in it.'

'What a gorgeous place to explore!'

'That's the trouble; it's very attractive, but you might have the roof fall in on you or you could get lost. So don't try to go inside.'

Peg went off on Pippin.

Robin and Adrian decided to take another look at the Pool and perhaps try their luck again at fishing if things were back to normal. They walked all round the water's edge, paddling barefoot across the dam at the lower end.

Adrian was relieved to find no dead fish. The large trout that had rolled over as if in great distress was not to be seen, so presumably had recovered, and the rest of the pond looked very much as usual – or nearly so. The water was quite clear now, but although there were fish to be seen they were not rising and there were no mayflies flitting over the surface.

The boys put their fishing-rods together and cast their artificial flies to trout lying motionless and uninterested.

'It's no good,' said Adrian at last; 'they're watching our every move in this bright light.'

They tried the shallows at the top end of the Pool, where a big willow cast some dappled shade. There was more movement of the water here, and ripples on the surface made it more difficult for trout to see the anglers but equally difficult for the anglers to see the trout. They tried other flies from Adrian's tin box, but with no success.

Altogether it was a reassuring but disappointing morning, and they returned to Up-hill Farm at lunch-time empty-handed.

Peg had come back from her ride. She and Helen had

just finished watering Pippin and now turned the pony into Five-acre with Grimaldi.

Christopher Bairstow came in from the farm yard and joined them. They washed and tidied themselves, then sat down at the big oak table, where Mary had a meal ready.

It was Mary who opened the conversation. 'Did you have a good ride, Peg?' she asked.

'Yes, thank you, Aunt Mary. Pippin and I went up the lane and turned left at the crossway along the grassy track, as Helen told me. At first it was a pretty glade with oak trees on either side. There were little rabbits frolicking and nibbling, and they didn't scatter until we came right up to them. It was like a beautiful painting, and I shouldn't have been at all surprised to see wood nymphs and shepherds dancing. I decided that I must have walked Pippin at least a mile, so it was time for a canter.'

'Did you go up to Bradbury Castle?' Helen asked.

'Yes, we forked left and went up the hill. It was lovely, going up there – so many wild flowers and butterflies. The foxgloves and red campions are nearly all over, but there are wild roses and scabious and harebells all along the hillside. I tied Pippin to a little ash tree while I had a closer look, and – can you believe it? – I found thirty different sorts of flowers.'

'You found a good spot,' Christopher agreed. 'It's too steep up there to be ploughed or cut for hay, and it's never been sprayed or given artificial fertilizers, just left year after year to set seeds.'

'Then I rode up to the top and all round. I had a wonderful view.'

'On a clear day you can see into ten counties,' Mary remarked, 'or so people say. I can never tell where one county ends and the next begins.'

Peg continued: 'On the way down I saw a big hole in the hillside, so I tied Pippin up again while I had a look. It might have been an old quarry, but the bottom went down ever so steep. I wondered if it was a mine shaft.'

63

'That's the Swallock,' Christopher told her. 'At least, that's what people round here call it. I've also heard it called a swallow-hole, swallet or slocker. It's not man-made, it's a natural cavity formed over millions of years by weak acids in rain water dissolving the limestone. . . . Oh dear, there's the telephone. I'll answer it, it's sure to be for me. You must excuse me for a minute.'

Christopher left the table, but was gone for more than a minute, so missed what followed.

Peg resumed her story. 'I went down to the bottom of the hill and doubled back left at the fork. I went along towards the old quarry Helen mentioned, but it isn't quite as she said. There isn't a wire fence; it's an ugly fence of rusty corrugated iron sheets with jagged spikes cut in the top, and the gate is covered with corrugated iron too. I saw the notice board; it says, "Danger. Radioactivity. Keep out." I was edging Pippin up to the gate, to try and look over, when there was a loud honk from a motor horn right behind me. Pippin was frightened.'

'Pippin is used to tractors and well-behaved motor cars,' Helen told her, 'but a sudden blast from something she hadn't seen would frighten any pony.'

'I wonder you weren't thrown off – or were you?' put in Mary.

'No. I thought Pippin was going to shy and throw me off, but I kept her head reined back and pressed with my knees. She was really very good. And then I wheeled her round to let her know I was still in control.'

'Good pupil, good teacher,' Mary said. It was she who had taught Helen to ride.

Robin, who felt some responsibility for his sister, was annoyed by the incident. 'It was a rotten thing to blast a horn like that,' he asserted. 'The driver could have sounded his horn from further away if he wanted Peg to move, or he could just have called out. What sort of person was it, anyway?'

'It was a tall man. He got out, undid the padlock and chain on the gate, and drove in. He was towing a horse box, but I didn't see any horse in it. He closed and padlocked the gate behind him. I'd enjoyed being out on Bradbury Castle all by myself – no disrespect to Helen! – but now I felt it was time to come home.'

Adrian asked, 'What was the car like?'

'Black, a sort of sports car.'

'Did you see its number?'

'Yes, I did. It was something funny, like POP 123. Oh, I remember now: it was ALE . . . ALE 9876.'

Adrian's interest was aroused. 'I've seen it before. And the horse box. But what's this about radioactivity?'

'That's what it said on the notice board: "Danger. Radioactivity. Keep out."'

'I wonder if they are prospecting for uranium in the Treacle Mine.'

'The Treacle Mine?' Robin queried. 'Is that what you said, Adrian?'

Now it was Peg's turn to tell her brother that the name was just a Bincombe joke; but there really was a mine, a disused one that had been started by the Romans.

Then Christopher came back to the meal table. 'Sorry I've been so long,' he apologized. 'That was Sergeant Badger, just keeping in touch. He says if we hadn't found that number plate he would scarcely have known where to start.'

Peg couldn't help feeling proud, and her shining eyes showed it; but her uncle's next words sobered her.

'The number plate turned out to be a false one. That may explain why it hadn't been fixed on securely. The detective says that the vehicle licensing people seldom have complete information about what eventually happens to the many thousands of motor vehicles they register. Many cars and lorries and motor cycles have unknown graves rusting away in forgotten places. But he was able to find out that Peg's number plate was one of a pair that came off a car, not a lorry, that ended up in a breaker's yard near Hereford. He says it's given him a lead, and he hopes to tell us more later.'

When the meal was finished, and by combined efforts the clearing-away had been quickly disposed of, Adrian telephoned Sparky Harris. Again he was lucky in finding him at home. Sparky recognized his voice.

'It's you, Adrian. I'm glad you've rung me. I've just finished making up an outfit for your Geiger counter. Can you come along and pick it up some time?'

'May I come this afternoon? I think I may have a use for it.'

Helen had said that Robin might use her bicycle, and Adrian had lowered the saddle for him. Now the two boys free-wheeled down the hill and pedalled along the High Street to Sparky's shop.

'I found I had an old walky-talky set stored away at the back of the shop,' Sparky told them, 'and I've adapted it to your Geiger counter. It's a bit bulky by modern standards, but it's got a shoulder strap, so you can carry it around with you.'

He laid the outfit on his work bench.

'You plug the cable from the counter in here, and connect your headphones there. Then you turn it on, and you point the little window of the counter at whatever you think radiation may be coming from. If there is any radiation you should hear clicks in the headphones, and you can tell whether the radiation is strong or weak by counting the number of clicks per minute. I haven't been able to check it for sensitivity, because I haven't any radioactive material, but it will probably be all right for minerals, if that's what you want it for.'

'Thank you for taking so much trouble, Mr Harris. Do I owe you a lot?' Adrian wondered how many months' pocket money must be put aside for his new acquisition.

Sparky stroked his right ear. 'I'll lend you the outfit,' he said, 'if you promise to take care of it; but I'd like you to pay for the batteries, as they cost me money to buy. Let me know how you get on.'

So it was arranged. Robin slung Sparky's apparatus across one shoulder, Adrian put the Geiger counter carefully back in his pocket, and they made their way back to Up-hill Farm as quickly as the steep hill would allow, scarcely noticing Anthracite, who was silently hunting the hedgerow for field mice.

Adrian rushed upstairs for his headphones, then they fetched from the pantry the two bottles of water they had collected in Adrian's wellington boots that morning. Breathless, they plugged in the cables and turned the apparatus on.

Robin grasped the neck of the first bottle in his left hand and took most of the weight with his right hand underneath, while Adrian moved the Geiger counter over the glass surface.

'It works! I can hear clicks!' Adrian shouted with delight. He listened attentively. 'I seem to get more clicks near the top of the bottle and hardly any at the bottom. Turning the knob makes the clicks louder or softer, but it doesn't seem to make any difference to how many clicks there are. Here, Robin, you listen.'

He took off the headphones and placed them over Robin's ears, then continued to move the Geiger counter up and down and around the bottle.

'Yes, you're right,' responded Robin. 'I can hear the clicks, but not all the time. When you put the counter near the bottle I hear some clicks, and when you move it away the clicks stop, so the water in the bottle must be radioactive – which is what you suspected.'

Robin put down the bottle and picked up the second. He held it up while Adrian resumed the headphones and scanned it in the same way as the first – with similar results.

Adrian put the headphones on Robin again. Robin listened. 'Yes, but no clicks near the bottom,' he said.

After a little more experiment they switched off and put the second bottle down. Since morning some greyish sediment had settled in the bottom of each bottle, but they had paid no attention to it; now they did.

'You'd expect it to be the sediment that gives the clicks,'

said Adrian at last, 'but it seems to be the other way round.'

'Perhaps the sediment makes an anti-click,' Robin suggested. 'I mean it stops the water from clicking.'

Adrian paused to consider this novel explanation. 'That could be it!' he said at last. 'If the clicks are caused by electrically charged particles, then the sediment might be carrying opposite charges to neutralize them. As for the fish and all the other animal life in the Pool, I think they were all suffering from radiation sickness this morning.'

'Why only this morning?'

'Somebody has been prospecting for uranium, and has disturbed radiation locked up in the rocks. Then the underground water picked it up, and it has got into the Bin Brook through the headsprings, and that's how the fish have been affected. We saw a grey cloud drifting down the Pool when everything was in commotion, remember. We don't know what damage has been done, nor whether it will happen again.'

The conclusion was mind-boggling.

'I hope we don't get radiation sickness too,' Robin said.

They put the bottles back in the pantry, dismantled the Geiger apparatus, carried the parts upstairs and stored them carefully in Adrian's bedroom.

'We must go and find out more of what Peg saw this morning,' Adrian decided. 'What is happening at the Treacle Mine? Let's go straightaway. Come on.'

They rushed downstairs and out of the back door, jumped on the bikes, and again pedalled as fast as the hill would let them, up to the crossway, then left along the green track, past the bridle path going up to Bradbury Castle, and so to the disused quarry. There was the corrugated iron fence with the jagged top, and there was the notice board, newly painted, saying, 'Danger. Radioactivity. Keep out.'

They heard a motor car approaching and instinctively looked for cover. The obvious place was down another green track opposite the quarry; it was overgrown, but because the woodland hereabout had been cleared of trees at some time they had to go at least fifty yards for any cover to be dense enough to hide themselves and their cycles. Even so, their only screen was a thin one of rosebay willow-herb. As they flung themselves flat on the ground a cock pheasant flew up vertically from nearby with a noisy flutter of wings and raucous double alarm call: *A-took, a-took!*

The boys wondered if they had been detected. A trickle of blood appeared on Adrian's face where in his haste he had scratched himself on brambles. As they watched and waited, the quarry gate was opened, the black Perugi Six emerged, still drawing the horse trailer, and a tall figure got out of the car, closed and chained the gate, re-entered the car and drove off toward the crossway and Westover.

Adrian and Robin grinned with relief.

Farther down the overgrown track was a large timber-framed shed. It had a good roof of pantiles, and three of its sides had been clad with corrugated iron, but most of the sheets were now missing. Inside the boys could see what looked from a distance like a steam roller and a work bench. As soon as the coast was clear Robin rushed to inspect closer. Adrian followed more slowly.

'This is, or used to be, the timber yard,' he told Robin. 'There's the circular saw, under that section of motor tyre, and over there are the chains and shackles they used for hauling big logs.'

'Oh, but look! It's a traction engine,' Robin exclaimed with glee. 'What a beauty!' First he walked all round it; then he clambered up on the steering chains to peer closely at the valve gear and governor as though he could scarcely believe his eyes; finally he climbed up from the back on to the footplate and with a faraway look seized the steering wheel. 'It's a Bowdler's Apollo!' he shouted. He was obviously thrilled.

'Well, we can't stop and play with it now,' Adrian

retorted with less enthusiasm. 'You can do that some other time. We still have serious work to do.'

'What's that, then?'

'We're not likely to get into the Treacle Mine easily through that gate or over the fence. But there's another entrance half a mile further along. Let's try and find it.'

Robin came down to earth reluctantly, still fancying himself driving a real steam traction engine. The two boys pushed their bicycles up the slope to rejoin the main track, then remounted and cycled on. After half a mile, as Adrian had expected, they came to a place where the hillside rose on their left in a rocky scarp hung with long skeins of ivy and traveller's joy. Behind a tangle of elder bushes they found a square opening hewn in the rock face. There had been a stout door-frame and a door of elm boards, but these had been smashed by the fall of an ancient stag-headed oak tree, whose huge bulk now blocked all entry.

Adrian pushed his way through the elder bushes and tried to squeeze between the door-post and the thick limbs of the oak tree, but presently disentangled himself and stood back to survey the problem.

'This is hopeless,' he said at last. 'That tree must weigh several tons, and we'll never be able to saw it into pieces.'

Sadly they picked up their bicycles and returned to Up-hill Farm.

Helen and Peg had just returned from a ride through the village. When the boys told them what they had been doing that afternoon, the girls were not so much interested in the Geiger counter as in the significance of the results.

'There must be radioactivity,' said Peg, 'and that's what upset your fish.'

'It may not be so simple as that,' said Helen. 'We must have a council of war and talk everything over. In the barn, this evening.'

9

In the barn

The barn was stacked high with bales of hay, mostly of ryegrass and clover, but some had been cut from old meadows rich in wild herbs that now gave off a delicious odour.

There was a long wooden ladder leading from ground level to the top of the stack. Helen, Adrian, Robin and Peg had climbed up and moved some of the bales to make a circle of seats between the queen-post roof trusses. Shep too had managed to scramble up there and now lay with his head pillowed on Peg's ankles.

'There's something going on,' Helen began, 'something that is not quite right. And we've got to find out what it is.'

'How much do we know already?' asked Robin.

'We think there is a man, probably two men, prospecting for radioactive minerals in the Treacle Mine,' Adrian replied. 'They obviously want to keep other people out and are trying to frighten away anyone like us. We don't like them, but we've nothing against them except that we think they are disturbing radioactive deposits. They are probably firing explosives to extract samples. That's what has given everything in Bincombe Pool an attack of radiation sickness. It could happen again and might be worse next time.'

'We could get radiation sickness ourselves,' Robin reminded them.

'What about Danny?' asked Helen.

'You don't believe he's got radiation sickness, do you?' Adrian countered. 'How could he get it? No, he's just had a tummy upset or something of that sort.'

'Haven't you heard?' Helen persisted. 'There were lots of people in Bincombe had upsets this morning. Doctor Hobday's surgery was crowded. We heard about it in the village this afternoon.'

'That only shows it's a germ going round – 'flu or something like that.'

Helen suddenly looked startled.

'It may not be radioactivity at all,' she said. 'Radioactivity may just be a blind. Why are they so secretive? Those rotters may be making explosives – bombs perhaps. What's going in and out in that horse box? They may even be breeding bacteria or viruses for germ warfare. If a few germs escaped, wouldn't that explain everybody going to the Doctor? I don't suppose they are doing whatever it is for our Government, not in that hole-and-corner way, and if it's not for the Government, then who? They could be anarchists, terrorists . . . we don't know.'

'Remember the Geiger counter,' Adrian insisted. 'That proves it's radioactivity at the bottom of the trouble. How lucky I found that thing at Aladdin's Cave!' He looked at his sister and pulled a funny face.

'Hadn't we better leave it to grown-ups – policemen and doctors and people like that – to find out what's wrong?' Peg interposed.

'That's all very well,' replied Robin, 'but other people don't notice what's going on. At least we've seen something and we do know a bit of what's happening. After all, what does the death of a few fish mean to most people? I don't suppose anyone really cares. If we go to the police or Doctor Hobday and tell them what we have seen and what we think, they will pooh-pooh it and we shall look very silly.'

'We don't know much – not yet,' Helen said. 'But we've

72

got to find out more. The question is: how?'

'We've got to get inside the Treacle Mine to suss out what's going on there,' Adrian said firmly. 'There's not much chance of getting in at the quarry entrance, whether it's over the tall corrugated iron fence with spikes on top or through the gate with its chain and padlock. Robin and I have looked at the other entrance, further along the ride. We might have got in there, but it's completely blocked by a fallen oak tree, much too big to saw up.'

'Can't you get in down the Swallock?' Peg asked innocently.

'That's an idea worth considering,' Helen admitted. 'It has been done – by some cavers from the University, fully kitted out with miners' equipment. But I don't know if we could do it.'

'What sort of equipment?' Adrian asked.

'Helmets, lamps, overalls, gumboots, ropes, I suppose,' Helen suggested.

'We could find all those things ourselves.'

'Iron bars, picks and shovels, perhaps,' Helen added.

'We're not going digging,' Robin reminded her. 'All the same, it will be dark and wet and very uncomfortable. Unlike the cavers, we will have to creep up secretly to find out what's going on. We mustn't be seen or make any noise.'

'Don't cavers use breathing apparatus?' Peg asked. 'I saw some on television with frogman suits and oxygen bottles.'

'That's only when they're exploring under water,' Robin told her. 'We don't want to do that.'

For a few moments they each followed their own thoughts.

'Who's game to try?' Adrian asked suddenly.

'I am,' came the answer, in chorus.

'And so am I. Time may be precious, so we must do it tomorrow morning.'

'We don't know how long it might take, so we'd better take lunch packets,' Helen advised. 'There's one more

73

thing,' she added. 'When we go riding, and especially if Peg goes out on her own, we must take Shep with us.'

The others nodded in agreement.

At the end of the meeting they all climbed down the ladder – all, that is, except Shep, who remained at the top, alternately barking and whining. It needed all of Helen's strength, aided by Robin above and Adrian below, to grasp him and descend the ladder again without falling over backwards.

10

A telephone call

Adrian was in the farm workshop early that Wednesday to get things ready for the day's expedition to the Swallock. Remembering his implied promise to Sparky, he had finally decided against taking the Geiger counter apparatus in case of damage, but had resolved to collect some rock specimens in the Treacle Mine and bring them home for testing. There were other things to take with him. He selected the longest rope from among the hanks, now hanging on the wall, that were used for tying loads on to wagons. Some discarded lengths of binder twine caught his eye and he picked them up. He felt the weight of a sledge hammer but decided it was too awkward and heavy to take, so chose a brick hammer for chipping off rock specimens.

He was about to go for breakfast, when he heard a motor engine and saw a blue motor van on the other side of the lane, pulled up by the Meter House. He found the driver in the Meter House doorway.

'Good morning,' Adrian began politely. 'Are you from the Water Board?'

The man nodded.

'Have you been flushing any mains here in the last day or so?'

It was the Water Inspector, and he looked at Adrian quizzically. 'No,' he replied after a pause. 'There's a main runs from here down to the trunk main in the valley, but if there's any flushing it's done down there, beyond Bincombe; not very often, either. What's the trouble, then?'

Adrian told him of the previous day's disturbance of the fishing. The Water Inspector listened understandingly. 'You can rest assured we haven't done anything to the Bin Brook that could affect your fishing,' he said.

Adrian caught sight of a notice on an inner door: 'Wear your gas mask.' He pointed and asked, 'What does that mean? You aren't wearing a gas mask.'

The man laughed. 'That applies when we are changing a chlorine cylinder. There have to be two of us in case of accidents. I come up once a week to change the charts on the meters and check that the chlorinator is working. If there was a leak you'd smell it as soon as you opened the front door.'

'So you use chlorine up here?'

'A very low dose to sterilize the drinking water. We don't chlorinate anything that overflows to the brook, only what goes into the main.'

Adrian persisted in his questions until he was fully assured that nothing the Walden Water Board had done could possibly have affected the fish in Bincombe Pool. He told the Water Inspector about the Geiger counter and the two bottles of water he had collected in his wellington boots. 'If nothing else has poisoned the fish I suspect they were suffering from radiation sickness. I've still got the bottles; I'll fetch them.'

He ran across the lane to the farm house and quickly reappeared with the samples of water.

The Water Inspector read the labels. 'I could take these back to our Chief Chemist,' he said. 'He could test them. I'll tell him what you say about the fish and the radioactivity.'

'Yes, please do.'

'Who shall I say sent them?'

'Adrian Bairstow, Up-hill Farm, Bincombe.'

Adrian handed the bottles over, then went into the farm

76

house for breakfast. The blue van presently departed.

☆ ☆ ☆

Christopher was reluctant to let Danny have anything to do with milking when he turned up for work that morning, in case he was incubating an infectious disease. This suspicion was strengthened by Danny himself.

'Oi weren't the only one took funny yesterday,' Danny said. 'There was lots of people down in the village took ill. It's some new bug goin' round, mebbe.'

'D'you feel all right now?'

'Oh yes, Boss. I have a good sleep when I get down home, and when I wake up in the afternoon I feel fine, but it were too late to come back to work.'

'You'd better keep away from the milk today and concentrate on the sheep. Have a look at their feet. We haven't checked them for foot rot since shearing. I'll bring you the antiseptic, and I'll come and help you when I've done the milking.'

At breakfast Christopher asked his daughter if she would again lend a hand in the dairy. Helen agreed somewhat reluctantly, then added, 'If Danny is attending to sheep and lambs I suppose he's using Shep.' Christopher nodded.

After breakfast Helen had a word with the others. 'If you go to Bradbury Castle, Peg can go on Pippin, and you boys on your bikes, but you'd better keep together,' she said. 'If you do go down the Swallock you must be very careful. Adrian can borrow my riding hat and Robin had better borrow Peg's, but she must have it back as soon as he's finished with it. I don't think Peg ought to go down. I'll join you as soon as I can get away.'

The cutting of sandwiches and checking of equipment delayed the start. At the last minute Robin decided to cycle down to Sparky's shop in the village to buy another electric torch, to supplement the big waterproof one that Adrian had already packed in his satchel. He had scarcely

77

got back when the telephone rang.

'It's the Water Board for you, Adrian,' said Mary, who had answered the ring. 'What they want I can't imagine. We're not on their main.'

Peg had already set out.

'You had better go on,' Adrian told Robin. 'I'll catch you up.' He picked up the telephone hand-set. 'Hallo,' he said.

'Is that Adrian Bairstow? My name is Derek Coleman; I am the Chief Chemist for Walden Water Board. You sent in two bottles of water by the Inspector this morning.'

'Yes.'

'He said you thought the water was radioactive and that radioactivity had caused some trouble with fish in Bincombe Pool. Is that right?'

'Yes.'

'Well, I've done a quick check for radioactivity and the result is negative. Can you tell me more?'

Adrian recounted the early-morning disturbance down at the Pool and began a long explanation of the new notice at the quarry and how he had used his own Geiger counter to scan the water samples.

The Chief Chemist interrupted. 'Do you wear a wrist-watch?'

'Yes, usually.'

'Has it got a luminous dial – hands and figures, that is?'

'No.'

'We won't pursue that, then. Anyway, I'd like to examine your samples further. It's my job to keep a check on water going into supply, and I like to know what ever is going on. I've already measured the dissolved oxygen in your samples: about seventy per cent in both bottles; nothing significant in that, except to know that your fish were not suffocated. There's some light sediment in the bottom of the bottles. Can I take it that it really is the cloudy matter you saw drifting across the Pool, not just dirt out of your wellington boots? . . . Oh, you washed one of your wellies out first, but not the other. There doesn't seem to be much difference, so I assume both boots were clean. Well, thanks for your help.'

He rang off abruptly, leaving Adrian a little bewildered but rather pleased that what he had done had been taken notice of.

As Adrian passed the dairy, Shep crossed his path. Adrian jumped off his cycle to find his father.

'Doesn't Danny want Shep any more?'

'It's all right; Danny has finished with him for the time being.'

So Shep and Adrian set off at last to catch up with Peg and Robin.

As he climbed the hill, Adrian turned over in his mind the telephone conversation with the Chief Chemist. Why was the Chief Chemist's check for radioactivity negative? Perhaps he didn't have so good a Geiger counter at the Water Board laboratory. Was Adrian's own Geiger counter OK or did it give clicks when it shouldn't? Perhaps that was why it had been disposed of to Aladdin's Cave. Sparky hadn't actually been able to test it with radioactive material. And what was that about a watch – a watch with a luminous dial? 'We won't pursue that, then.'

Adrian's watch wasn't luminous, but Robin's was.

A horrible suspicion entered Adrian's mind. The more he thought about it the worse it became. Could the luminous figures on Robin's watch have caused the clicks in the Geiger counter?

11

The Swallock

It was a beautiful summer morning under a wide blue sky
flecked by only a few small fleecy clouds. Peg was
thoroughly enjoying her ride up the hill on Pippin.
Everyone had to carry something, and she was entrusted
with a rucksack containing lunch packets amd thermos
flasks.

Reaching the bridle path that led up to Bradbury Castle,
she started looking for any wild flowers that she had not
noticed on her previous ride there. She was rewarded by
the sight of some pale purple orchids. On jumping down
from Pippin to look closer she decided it was the sort
called common spotted orchid; farther over she saw there
were thinly scattered drifts of it.

'Not so common nowadays,' she told herself. 'I suppose
it's called common because there's another spotted
orchid, very like it but not so common, that grows on peaty
moors.'

Nearby she found twayblades growing. She did not wish
to pick any of the flowers but resolved to tell Uncle Chris
she had found them, and to come back another day in
order to make a sketch.

Pushing his bicycle up the slope, Robin presently
caught up with her. He carried a rucksack filled with
waterproof clothing, woollen pullovers, towels, Helen's
riding hat and his new torch. Then Shep came bounding
along, followed by Adrian, who had the coil of rope round

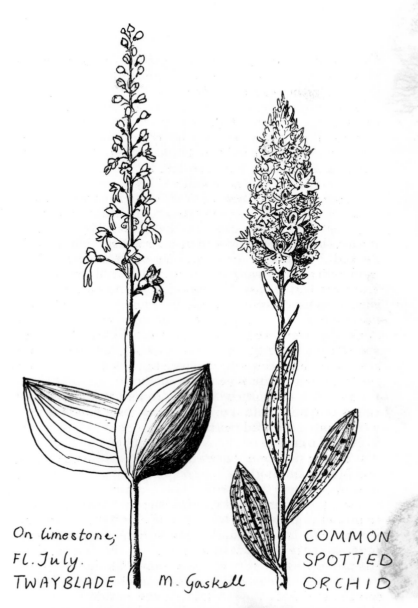

On limestone;
Fl. July.
TWAYBLADE

M. Gaskell

COMMON
SPOTTED
ORCHID

When Peg went back to the Bradbury Castle bridle path,
to make a sketch, this was the result.

81

his shoulders. Slung along the cross-bar of his cycle was his school satchel containing the hammer, his pocket knife, the binder twine and his big torch.

Both boys were already dressed in jeans and wellingtons. Arrived at the mouth of the Swallock, Peg tethered Pippin to a nearby ash tree and the boys put on their pullovers and waterproofs and topped them with the riding hats as Helen had instructed.

The entrance to the Swallock lay in a hollow that collected rain water from the near side of Bradbury Castle. At the moment it was dry, but they could hear the sound of water running in the dark depths below. The Swallock started as a downward slope, then appeared to drop down vertically – just how far down they could not tell. There were no trees growing close around the entrance, and Adrian was at a loss for something to tie the rope to. Finally, some distance away, he found a branch of a whitebeam tree, probably torn off in a winter gale. He dragged it along, wedged it across the top of the Swallock, and to make sure the rope wouldn't slip he tied a clove hitch and finished it with two half-hitches; then he threw the loose end of the rope down the hole.

The boys slung their torches round their necks by means of binder twine, so as to leave their hands free.

'Let me go down first and see if the rope is long enough,' Robin volunteered.

'It's a good long one, but be prepared to climb up again if you don't touch bottom.'

Robin grasped the rope and lowered himself slowly, his feet and legs in close contact with the rope to act as brakes except when he needed to fend himself off the rocky side or search for a foothold. At first Adrian shone his torch down the hole to aid Robin's progress, then realized he was probably only causing dazzle and that Robin's eyes could quickly become accustomed to the gloom. Robin disappeared from view. Adrian waited beside Peg.

'It's OK,' came Robin's voice presently. 'I've reached a flattish place, but there's water in it, quite a stream in fact.

82

You can come on down. There's plenty of rope.'

Adrian gave Peg a few last-minute instructions. 'Give us an hour,' he said. 'Here, you'd better take my watch.' He passed his wrist-watch over and saw Peg strap it on her wrist two holes tighter than when he wore it. 'If you get bored you can eat some sandwiches, but don't scoff the lot; we shall be hungry when we come up. If we aren't back in an hour, shout down the hole and listen for an answer; if you don't get an answer, wait ten more minutes and shout again. If you still don't get an answer you had better ride down to the farm and tell Helen.'

He scrambled into the mouth of the Swallock and let himself down the rope.

Down below, Robin's torch showed a water-worn channel floored with grey gravel and lime-encrusted boulders, some of them bigger than a sheep. Sides and roof were of wet limestone. Water in the channel lay two or three feet deep in pools, but elsewhere it was shallow.

When Adrian finished his descent the two boys picked their way by the dim light of their torches, proceeding downstream, squeezing between obstructions, clambering over others. Above their heads the roof was irregular, spangled in places with short straw-stalactites that dripped cold water on their faces if they looked up. Their riding hats saved them from bumps on the head, but staggering on in places where they could not stand upright made their backs and thighs ache, and it was almost a relief when they came to a place where the natural roof was so low that they could proceed only on hands and knees. Doing this meant crawling in water, however, and they soon found that they were soaking wet right up to their necks.

Something unseen brushed close to Robin's face like a puff of cold air.

'What's that?' he cried, startled.

Adrian too had felt it. 'It must be a bat,' he said. 'I've heard that horseshoe bats live in underground tunnels like this.'

83

'Do they suck blood?'

'Only vampire bats suck blood, and we haven't any of those in this country. Ours mostly eat insects.'

Robin again thought Adrian sounded a little conceited about his knowledge of natural history, so he asked, 'Have you heard why the barn owls in the Lake District haven't paired up this year?'

'I didn't know they hadn't. Why haven't they?'

'It's too-wet-to-woo!'

If Robin had hoped this would leave Adrian speechless he was mistaken, for his cousin laughed and at once came back at him: 'You mean brown or tawny owls; they are the ones that are supposed to say *tu-whit, tu-woo*. Barn owls screech; we hear them at the farm. Helen says they cry *Wilfred! You're wicked!*'

Robin could see that he had only scored an own goal, and it was silly to be envious of Adrian's country lore. Anyway, he had learned something about owls.

It was difficult to hold a conversation against the noise of the rushing water, and both boys fell silent while they continued to force their way through deep pools and scramble over boulders. Once Robin slipped and in saving himself let go of his new torch. Fortunately the light stayed on, so although the torch was carried several feet downstream by the current he was able to regain it at the cost of dipping down till his face was right under water.

At last they reached a place where the natural channel had been improved by the work of miners. From there on they were able to walk upright in a rough-hewn tunnel, the water running in a sizeable stream on their right, with rivulets joining it at irregular intervals.

They went on for several hundred yards; it was difficult to measure distance. Then, rounding a slight bend in the tunnel, they saw some light ahead; not the whiteness of daylight but a faint yellowish glow. Above the gurgling of the stream they became aware of a deeper splashing noise and a sort of pulsation. They also noticed a strange smell: not a river smell but a mixed odour like rotting cabbages,

84

vinegar and ammonia. They switched off the torches and proceeded cautiously, feeling their way along the left-hand wall of the tunnel.

Ahead of them they made out a natural cave, some sixty feet across, its walls like beaten metal curtained with folds of limestone in grey, pink and mauve. Stalactites hung glistening from the uncertain blackness of an unseen roof; tapering stalagmites rose from below, some of them joining the stalactites to form columns. The floor of the cave lay ten feet or so below the tunnel they were in and sloped away to the right, where it was lapped by a lake that mirrored the waxy stalactites and stretched away into darkness.

Adrian cupped his hands over Robin's ears. 'This must be the Roman Cavern,' he told him.

The boys could see a steep ramp on their left and some steps cut into it leading down to the Cavern floor from the tunnel mouth where they now crouched. But what amazed them most was the result of some very recent human activity: the scene was lit by electric lights hanging on wires slung across the Cavern from column to column. The lamp bulbs were not powerful or numerous enough to illuminate everything there, but they revealed some surprising objects.

The source of the rushing noise and pulsation could now been seen: a rotating water wheel. It was geared to a shaft carrying a number of pulley wheels. One of them was connected by a belt to an electric generator; this explained the electric lighting in a situation far from public power lines. A belt drive from another pulley led to a root-cutter, the sort of machine Adrian's father used for chopping up turnips fed to cattle. Close by was a heap of large white, mauve and yellow vegetables that Adrian recognized as swedes, and just beyond them was a wheelbarrow.

The whole scene was like a theatre set, and arranged about the floor of the Cavern, like stage properties, was a mixed assemblage of apparatus. Near the boys, on the right, a water tank had been erected on a framework of sawn logs. On the left, supported by tubular scaffolding, was a battery of what looked like huge glass flasks connected to ducting; the flasks were heated by burners fed from gas bottles. Under a bright cluster of electric lights stood a long wooden work-bench on which lay some large stainless-steel basins, laboratory glassware, a pair of household scales with brass pans and weights, and a rack of stoppered bottles. Scattered around in half-shadow were vague boxes, carboys and a white bin-like object that might have been a centrifuge.

On the far left of the Cavern the boys observed a black hole, possibly the way into another tunnel. A little nearer Adrian noticed an old-fashioned cider press, a long ladder and the Tyer's oil furnace, which was alight and added a roar to the general noise; they could see that it was heating an open pan from which vapour was rising.

Moving centre-stage were two actor-like figures: a stout man in a stained white overall, and a tall, rather stooping man in what looked like a nylon raincoat. Adrian recognized them at once as the pair he had seen with the Perugi Six and green horse trailer at Aladdin's junk-shop. The tall man was attending to the oil furnace. As the boys watched they saw the stout man tip a barrowload of swedes into a tub, stir them round as if to wash off mud, and feed them with a wire scoop into the hopper of the root-cutter.

From up in the gallery Robin and Adrian could not hear or see all that was taking place on the stage, but above the noise of the water wheel they caught broken snatches of conversation.

'. . . Keep that pan stirred. If you let it stick again there'll be another batch down the sink . . . your fault, remember.'

'I don't like this furnace thing.' It was the tall man speaking now. 'You can't expect me to stir and pump at the same time.'

'. . . better than the bottle gas . . . wish you'd do your share of the work and not leave it all to me.'

86

'Leave it all to you? I've raised the lolly, haven't I? We'd never have got off the ground without it. It's only a few weeks since we were both inside, remember. My speciality is finance, not being a dogsbody. I reckon I've done remarkably well to raise all the money in so short a time.'

'It's easy to find people willing to risk their money for a fat profit. That's human cupidity.'

They saw the stout man move over to the bench and measure into a conical glass flask a golden liquid that caught the radiance of the electric light; then he let down into it another liquid from a glass burette, shaking the flask as he did so. Like a conjurer's trick, the golden tint changed to purple.

The tall man pumped up the oil furnace, and the dialogue was drowned for a while in the ensuing roar. Next they heard:

'. . . old skinflint knows they're difficult to come by at this time of year. He says we'll have to pay him more. We may have to wait for the new crop, and that'll be some time . . .'

Again the conversation became inaudible, but presently they caught some more of it: '. . . silly enough to write cheques in this game. You'll have to watch it the notes aren't forged.'

'I rang the Octopus and told him we'd have the first lot ready for him on Sunday night: nine o'clock at old Friend's, where we met before.'

'You didn't tell him it's nerrowin'?'

'I'm not as daft as that.'

There was more noise; then it abated temporarily and they heard: '. . . Junkies never know what they're getting. It's usually cut with lactose or some . . .'

The roar of water and appliances swelled like the sound of a great organ. When it receded the voices had petered out.

The boys were about to make a move, but then they heard more conversation and pricked up their ears.

'. . . girls on ponies and boys on bikes.'

'You should have known if you tell people to keep out their curiosity will be aroused and they'll try to get in.'

'We can't afford to let them interfere.'

'What do you propose to do, then?'

'If they become a nuisance we'll have to eliminate them.'

'How can we do that?'

'The Octopus will know . . .'

The many noises once more built up into a wall of sound that effectively cut off further listening.

Robin shifted his cramped limbs, and his torch made a clatter against the hard rock. The boys held their breath, fearing the sudden sound out in the darkness might call attention to their presence. But the men in the Cavern, surrounded by noise, appeared to have heard nothing unusual.

Robin looked at his watch and motioned to Adrian that it was time to go. They started to move back along the tunnel, but it was not easy because they dared not use their torches, and the faint glow coming from the electric lights in the Cavern only threw shadows on the path of retreat. They inched their way, feeling along the rock wall now on their right, but there were side galleries and gaps that left them groping blindly. When they reached the bend, and looking back no longer saw the glow from the Cavern, they deemed it safe to use their torches, and did so to speed their progress.

Repeatedly they found themselves splashing through water; elsewhere the floor was muddy and slippery. Adrian slipped and came down heavily, but Robin helped him up and they went on. After a while Robin stopped and grasped Adrian's sleeve. They were still in the man-made tunnel, but shining their torches around they sensed they were not in that part of it they had come along previously. For a moment each felt he was lost; it was a fearful situation.

In a low voice Robin said, 'We've overshot where we

came in.'

'This tunnel must go on to the other entrance, the one that's blocked by the oak tree,' Adrian agreed. 'We'd better go back.'

They started to retrace their steps. There were several openings off the tunnel; to find the right one was a vital problem.

'If we can't find where we came into this tunnel we might try getting out by the other tunnel, beyond the Roman Cavern,' Robin whispered. 'That must be the way the men come and go between the Roman Cavern and the quarry. It's probably a better passage than this, because that must be how all the apparatus was brought into the Cavern – and all in the wheelbarrow.'

'That way is no good to us,' Adrian argued. 'First we'd have to get past the men in the Roman Cavern without being seen. And even if we got out at the far end we'd still have to get over the corrugated iron fence with spikes.'

'It would be easier to climb over from inside than from outside.'

'Even so, I don't think that way out sounds very easy for us – too many uncertainties, and we've no time left. Peg will be getting worried.'

'There are uncertainties this way. But I s'pose you're right.'

'We'd better try the most likely places along this tunnel one at a time, but not both of us together in case we get lost; one of us must stay in this tunnel until the other signals he's found the right route. You stay here, Robin, with your torch, while I try this passage.'

Adrian clambered into a large opening, but in a minute he was back. 'That's not the way.'

They retreated a little farther.

'I'll try this one.' Once more Adrian left Robin and explored the darkness, but he returned.

'That's no good either. We must go back until we pick up our footmarks – where there are prints pointing towards the Roman Cavern. Better still, only one of us should do it,

89

to avoid confusing the trail.'

'I'll try this time,' Robin volunteered, and off he went, shining his torch on the floor of the tunnel while Adrian followed slowly behind him, keeping a distance.

'OK,' Robin called. 'It's here.'

Adrian rejoined him, looked at the footprints, then at the opening Robin had found, and agreed this was where they had first come into the man-made tunnel.

The light of Adrian's torch had faded to a glimmer. He switched it off to rest the batteries, but his progress and Robin's too became slower. On hands and knees they groped their way upstream between boulders in the channel down which they had originally come. Going upstream was easier than coming down, but they were getting very tired. Wherever the roof was higher they were able to straighten their knees but they still had to bend their backs, and O how their backs ached!

'What's the time?' Adrian asked.

Robin looked at his watch again, a tiny dial of little green figures glowing in the darkness. 'We've had well over an hour,' he answered.

'Peg will be getting worried,' Adrian said. 'I hope she doesn't panic.'

They resumed their weary journey, stumbling more or less forward and upward. The going was a little easier now. At last they were rewarded by sight of a glimmer of daylight ahead. They kept on until, wet and tired, they reached the rope at the bottom of the Swallock.

'Hallo, there!' they shouted together, knowing they were now too far away for loud voices to be heard back in the Roman Cavern.

Scarcely waiting for a reply, Adrian seized the rope and began to climb. He was only a few feet up when Robin started to follow. There was a faraway cracking of dry wood, the rope slackened and they fell together into a rock pool, the rope snaking down on top of them.

12

Getting out

Up above, Peg had at first passed the time by making short journeys on Pippin. Shep raced round her, finding wild scents and chasing rabbits. Peg did not wish to go far from the Swallock, however, so she tethered Pippin and started looking for mushrooms, but without success. 'It's still too early in the summer,' she consoled herself.

Then some silver birch trees gave her an idea for passing the time, so she peeled off some strips of their loose papery bark. They were like scrolls of wood shavings. She took a pencil from her pocket, and resting a strip on the pony's saddle found that with care she could write on it. Calling Shep, she tried curling the bark round his collar and was pleased to find that it lay there snugly, but disappointed that on uncurling it the strip broke into pieces.

She looked at Adrian's watch and was annoyed with herself to find the time had gone quicker than she had expected. It was over an hour since Adrian went down the rope. She ran to the mouth of the Swallock.

'Hello, there!' she called. There was a faint echo but no answering hail. 'Robin! . . . Adrian! . . .'

She repeated her calls, feeling more and more horror-stricken as minutes passed, a good ten minutes.

Now she took a piece of birch bark and with unsteady hands wrote on it in block letters: 'BOYS LOST IN SWALLOCK. SEND HELP.' She curled it several times

91

round Shep's collar.

'Home, Shep!' she commanded, and pointed down the bridle path. At first Shep did not seem to understand. 'Home, Shep, home!' she repeated. 'You will get there quicker than I can.'

She ran a few paces with him, and he raced off down the hill.

Before mounting Pippin, Peg returned to the mouth of the Swallock and peered down. Above the gurgle of water far below she heard a faint shout: 'Hallo, there!' Her heart leapt with relief. Then there was a cracking sound; she saw the whitebeam branch break and the rope disappeared from her sight.

Peg shouted down the Swallock: 'Robin! Adrian! Are you all right?'

Their voices came up to her faintly: 'Yes, but the rope has fallen. We can't climb out.'

'What am I to do?'

'You'll have to ride down to the farm and get Helen to find another rope. Don't be long. We're very wet.'

Peg untethered Pippin and set off briskly down the hill.

To the waiting boys she seemed to be gone a very long time. They began to feel cold and very weary.

Robin thought of Arctic explorers who dozed off, overcome by cold, never to awaken. He wished he had asked Peg to throw some lunch packets down the Swallock, but surmised they would have lodged tantalizingly out of reach.

Adrian remembered his intention of collecting rock specimens. He had not brought the brick hammer down the Swallock in case it was an encumbrance, but had intended to bring it down on a second descent. Now he picked up a few rounded stones from the bed of the stream. While Robin shone his torch for him he tried using a small boulder as a hammer to break off fresh specimens of rock, but with little success. He reflected miserably on the doubtful result of testing the bottles of water for

92

radioactivity. There was something he must do about that: as soon as they returned home he must try the Geiger counter on Robin's wrist-watch, and perhaps get Robin to hold up an empty bottle in the same way as he had held the water samples, while he made a scan.

At last the boys heard Helen's voice from the top of the Swallock. Adrian had never noticed before what a pleasant voice she had.

'Hello! I'm letting a rope down, but don't put any weight on it until I tell you I've got it fixed.'

They saw the rope dangling above their heads but could not reach it.

'Let down some more.'

'I can't; it's all I've got.'

Robin tried climbing up the foot of the Swallock, but it was too wide and too steep, and he could not reach anywhere near the rope.

'There are two pieces of binder twine in my satchel on the bike,' Adrian called out. 'Tie them together and then to the top of the rope with a fisherman's knot.'

'Binder twine won't carry your weight.'

'You'd be surprised; but it won't need to. If you can let your rope down a little lower so that we can reach it we can tie our long rope on the bottom and you can haul it up.'

The boys waited while Helen sought and tied on the binder twine. Then the rope descended a few more feet, but its lower end was still out of reach.

'We still can't reach it,' they called.

'How much short are you?'

'Sorry, we can't hear.'

'How much are you short?'

'About five feet.'

There was a pause, then Helen's voice: 'I've an idea.' More faintly: 'Peg, fetch Pippin. I want her reins off, and you must hold her.'

The rope was withdrawn and there was another spell of waiting while Helen's deft fingers released Pippin's reins and joined them to the binder twine. Then the rope

93

descended again; its lower end reached the boys' waist level.

'Don't put any weight on this. Just tie your rope on and I'll pull it up.'

Adrian tied the long wet rope to the shorter dry one. 'OK. Haul away,' he shouted. The wet rope was whisked upward. Robin held its lower end until the movement stopped.

They heard Helen's voice: 'Wait a minute while we put Pippin's reins on and tie her up.'

On Peg's advice Helen had brought a fencing stake to wedge across the mouth of the Swallock, but now it proved too short for effectively securing the rope.

Helen called down, 'I've got a problem.'

Very faintly the boys heard Peg's voice: 'We could tie both ropes together securely and fix one to the tree where the ponies are tethered.'

There was yet another period of waiting until Helen shouted, 'Try this gently.'

Robin pulled on the lower end of the rope that he still held in his hand. There was some slack to be taken up, and when he eventually tried his weight on it the rope stretched slightly but held firm.

'Everything's all right at the top,' Helen called down the Swallock, 'so up you come, but only one at a time.'

Robin climbed the rope first. His muscles were cold and cramped, but he assisted his ascent by pushing on any ledges that his feet could find. Helen gave him a helping hand at the top, and he was soon followed by Adrian.

Peg had unpacked the thermos flasks and handed out full cups. Never had hot, sweet coffee tasted so good!

The fine weather of earlier in the day had turned windy and overcast while the boys were down the Swallock, but now the sun came out again from behind clouds. The four cousins found a sunny bank sheltered from the wind and sat relaxed, eating sandwiches and hard-boiled eggs and fruit.

'What did you find down the Swallock?' asked Helen at

last.

'The Roman Cavern was fantastic,' her brother replied. 'I've never seen such marvellous stalactites. But that wasn't all . . .'

'It was like that Flemish picture called *The Alchemist's Den,*' Robin interrupted. 'And there was even electric light . . .'

'I should say it was something between Imperial Chemical Industries and Heath Robinson's style of do-it-yourself.'

Dark clouds with silver edges blotted out the sun again; a few raindrops were carried by the wind; the air suddenly felt cold.

'You boys had better get home and changed,' Helen advised. 'You can tell us all about it this evening – in the barn.'

13

'*Sick of radioactivity*'

As soon as he had washed and changed completely into dry clothing, Adrian got out the Geiger counter, Sparky's amplifier and the headphones. He picked a shampoo bottle at random from the bathroom cupboard. Robin, likewise in dry clothes, joined him from across the landing.

'Would you mind holding up this bottle while I scan it with the Geiger counter?' Adrian asked. He plugged in the cables and turned the apparatus on.

They went through the same motions as they had with the two bottles of water the day before. It was soon evident that the clicks in the headphones originated from the luminous hands and figures of Robin's wrist-watch.

'The bottles of water from the Pool were not radioactive after all,' Robin commented. 'But at least you know now that your Geiger counter works.'

'Let's try the specimens of rocks.' Adrian produced the stones he had brought from the stream bed in the Swallock, and presented them one by one to the window of the Geiger counter. There were no responsive clicks in the headphones.

'I guess radioactivity is out,' he said at last. He switched off and unplugged the apparatus.

Robin coughed gently. 'Adrian,' he said solemnly, 'I am afraid you are suffering from radiation sickness.'

'Me? What ever do you mean? Why do you say that?'

'I'm sure you are *sick of radioactivity!*'

Adrian threw a wet sock at him. 'What you need,' he said, 'is a job in a Christmas-cracker factory, writing loony mottoes.'

☆ ☆ ☆

The evening was marked by wind and showers of rain, but up on the hay in the barn all was snug.

'I've a confession to make,' Adrian began. 'There's no radioactivity: not in the water, not in the rocks I brought back.' He explained how he had been misled by Robin's luminous wrist-watch.

'But there is something strange going on,' Robin pointed out. 'That notice board is just a bluff.'

'Not necessarily,' Helen rejoined. 'It's just that you haven't detected any radioactivity, which may be there nevertheless.' She was tempted to gloat over her brother's mistake; he had been rather cocky about his Geiger counter. But the matter was too serious to bicker about, so she said instead, 'Tell us what you saw down the Swallock.'

In turns the boys described how they had followed the stream at the foot of the Swallock until it led to a man-made tunnel and so to the Roman Cavern.

'It really was fantastic,' Robin told his listeners. 'Besides the great stalagmites and stalactites there was a clear blue-green lake, and the place was lit by electric lights.'

'It was kitted out like a chemical factory. It smelt like our chem'y lab. at school.'

'There were two men in overalls,' Robin continued.

'I'm sure they were the two that I saw at Aladdin's Cave, the junk-shop in Westover,' Adrian added.

'It was amazing how they'd rigged the place up. They must have spent weeks, perhaps months, doing it all.'

'They had a water wheel driven by the stream.'

'It looked like an overshot wheel that had been bolted

together in sections,' Robin explained.

'It was driving a generator that made the electricity.'

'Did you notice they had a portable generator too?' Robin asked Adrian. 'I reckon they used that while they were fixing up the water wheel and they kept it as a standby.'

'Some of the equipment was old-fashioned, but some of it looked very modern.'

'It sounds as though it must have cost a lot of money and effort,' was Helen's comment.

'That means they expect to make a lot of money,' Peg conjectured.

'Remember they had the green horse box to bring plant and equipment. If it had been a builder's lorry people would have wondered what was going on, but a horse box doesn't arouse suspicion in the country.'

'Never mind about how they set it all up,' Helen interrupted. 'What did you see the men actually doing?'

'While we were there one of them was chopping up swedes in a root-cutter.'

'I thought Swedes were people who live in Sweden,' Peg protested.

'I mean Swedish turnips. Farmers call them swedes. We grow them and feed them to cattle during the winter.'

'The other man was stirring something in a big shiny pot – stainless steel, I expect – with a burner underneath.'

'They could have been making turnip jam,' Peg suggested, half in jest.

'That's it,' laughed Robin. 'Imagine the label: "Walden Brand turnip jam. Made only with locally grown turnips and finest treacle from our own treacle mine." '

'Seriously, though,' said Helen, 'they might be making something patent, quite legally, and doing it in the Treacle Mine to keep it secret from the public or trade competitors.'

'I think they're a pair of crooks,' Robin said bluntly.

'What makes you think that?' Helen asked.

'Well, look at the way one of them frightened Pippin,'

Robin answered.

'That doesn't make them both crooks,' Helen reasoned. 'You could say it was just bad manners.'

'No, but we heard them talking,' Robin countered.

'There was a lot of noise in the Cavern,' Adrian explained, 'but now and again we caught a few words of conversation.'

Robin interrupted: 'I think they might have been quarrelling, because they raised their voices, and that's how we were able to hear so much in spite of the noise.'

Adrian continued: 'I overheard the short man say, "Keep that pan stirred. If you let it stick again there'll be another batch down the sink." There was a sink at the end of the work-bench, and I suppose it would drain straight into the lake.'

'Letting the pan stick reminds me of King Alfred and the burnt cakes,' Peg chipped in.

'There's a special meaning of "sink",' Helen suggested. 'It means the place where a watercourse disappears underground.'

'I don't suppose he was using it in that sense. But it's all the same,' Adrian reasoned; 'whatever was dumped would get into underground water and come out lower down at springs. That's how something got into the Bin Brook.'

'That wasn't the only thing we overheard,' Robin told the girls.

Adrian continued his account: 'I heard one of them say, "It's easy to find people willing to risk their money for a fat profit. That's human stupidity."'

Robin interrupted again. 'I think he said "cupidity", not "stupidity".'

'Did he?'

Peg asked, 'What is cupidity? Is it anything to do with Cupid?'

Helen answered, 'Yes and no. Cupidity is greedy desire for gain. "Cupid" and "cupidity" both come from a Latin word meaning "desire". Human cupidity is just selfish desire for riches.'

Adrian resumed: 'If big profits are expected, where will they come from? From selling what is being made at the Treacle Mine?'

Robin joined in again: 'It sounded as though they expect to receive some money soon for what they are making. And they want it in bank notes, not a cheque. I think that sounds fishy – as though whatever is going on is illegal.'

'Not necessarily. Cheques can bounce.' Helen was not wholly convinced. 'And they might only be dodging income tax.'

'That's illegal, isn't it?' Robin challenged.

'There was more to it than that,' Adrian hastened to add. 'One of them said, "You'll have to watch it the notes aren't forged." It sounds as if they're dealing with crooks, and they're all fiddling big money.'

'Thousands of pounds,' Peg suggested.

'Did you catch what the tall man said before that?' Robin asked. 'He said, "I've raised the lolly. It's only a few weeks since we were both inside, remember." "Inside" means in prison, so they must have been in gaol. I tell you they're crooks.'

Helen had to concede that Robin was right. 'But we don't know what it is these men are making,' she reminded the others. 'It seems it might be some sort of chemical.'

'We still haven't told you everything we overheard,' Robin went on. 'One of them said – I think it must have been the tall man – he said, "I rang the Octopus and told him we'd have the first lot ready for him on Sunday night, nine o'clock at old friends' where we met before." Who and where are their old friends? Then the other man said, "You didn't tell him it's narrowing." It might have been a question, because the first one replied, "I'm not as daft as that." '

'What is it that was narrowing?' Peg asked.

'I'm not sure if he said "narrowing",' Adrian answered. 'It sounded to me more like "nerrowing" with an *e*, but that may be the fancy way they speak, a sort of Kensington.'

'It all sounds very strange, as though they are concealing what they are doing, and hiding the truth from whoever it is they are doing it for,' Helen observed.

'That may well be so,' Robin replied, 'because the short man then said, "Junkies never know what they are getting." '

'What are junkies?' Peg inquired.

'They are something like hippies, aren't they?' Robin suggested.

'No,' Helen told them. 'Junkies are drug addicts.'

'What are addicts?' Peg persisted.

'Drug addicts are people who start taking drugs for kicks and then find it's become a habit and they can't give it up,' Helen explained. 'They go downhill horribly, all dirty and spineless.'

Peg thought for a moment, then she said, 'Perhaps we've got it. Suppose those men really are making drugs in the Treacle Mine; they will have some ready to sell to the Octopus on Sunday night when they meet up with their old friends.'

'We don't know what sort of drugs – if it is drugs, that is,' Helen said. 'We hear about all sorts of things – cannabis and amphetamines and LSD and lots of technical names that just mean nothing to us.'

'It doesn't matter to us what sort of drug. We only want to know how the fish were affected,' Adrian emphasized.

'I said they are crooks,' Robin reminded his audience. 'We are dealing with crooks, and they could be dangerous. They've already got it in for us.'

'What do you mean?' Helen looked sharply at Robin. 'None of your jokes, Robin.'

'They have noticed us around: "Girls on ponies and boys on bikes" one of them said. If we interfere with what they are doing or make ourselves a nuisance they will ask the Octopus how to eliminate us.'

'Eliminate us?' Helen repeated. 'I don't like the sound of that.'

'That's what we heard,' Adrian confirmed.

'Who or what is the Octopus?' was Helen's next question.

Robin coughed. 'The Octopus is a queer fish,' he jested.

Helen gave him a reproving look.

'An octopus isn't a fish, stupid,' Peg told him; 'it's a shellfish without a shell.'

'There you are then: a shellfish without a shell is a fish, isn't it?'

'No, it isn't. An octopus is a mollusc, and it's the cleverest of all the animals that have no backbones.'

'Well, the Octopus may not be a proper fish, but he's slimy and the whole business is fishy.' Then: 'Sorry, Helen,' Robin said. 'I can't help making silly jokes. Seriously, though, I reckon he's the Boss Man of the outfit.'

'We really must find out more about what you call the outfit. And before Sunday,' Helen insisted.

'Why before Sunday?'

'That's when they meet up. We must forestall them somehow. After our two have got together with the Octopus we don't know what they might try in order to eliminate us. Today is Wednesday, tomorrow will be Thursday, so we can't afford to waste any time.'

'We must all get into the Treacle Mine,' Peg affirmed. 'Then we can all give evidence and everybody really will believe us.'

'We mustn't go down the Swallock again,' Adrian warned. 'None of us must. It isn't safe. I realize now that if there had been a thunderstorm Robin and I might have been drowned. Looking back, I think we were foolhardy, but we didn't see it that way at the time. We can't afford to make mistakes.'

'You must have had a nasty shock when you read the message on Shep's collar,' said Peg. 'I thought Shep would get back quicker than I could, so it would save time in summoning help.'

'What message was that?' Helen asked. 'Shep came

running into the farm yard, but I didn't see any message on his collar.'

'I wrote on a strip of birch bark and curled it round Shep's collar: "Boys lost in Swallock. Send help." '

'I'm glad I didn't see it. I would have feared the worst.'

Shep was again lying on Peg's ankles. She leaned forward and rubbed him affectionately behind the cheek bones.

'Shep could be a useful messenger if needed,' Helen agreed; 'but we would have to use something better than birch bark. We need a few luggage labels in our rucksacks.'

Reclining comfortably on the bales of hay, each of them became lost in thought.

'I have an idea.' It was Robin who revived the conversation. 'If we could move the fallen oak tree we could get into the Treacle Mine by the far entrance. And if only that traction engine was working we could shift the tree with the winding gear.'

'Do you think we could?' asked Adrian, surprised at his cousin's initiative.

'Yes. You yourself pointed out the chains and shackles used for hauling heavy logs,' Robin reminded him. 'The trouble is that all the copper pipes have been wrenched off the traction engine and stolen.'

Adrian reflected. 'I might be able to do something about that. I've got some copper tube.'

'Do you mean those old pipes and fittings you rescued last year when we had a new central heating system?' Helen asked him.

'Yes,' Adrian replied. 'It's good stuff, better than they use nowadays.'

The conversation turned to how they could get the traction engine working. Robin was an enthusiastic reader of books about steam engines and he seldom missed an opportunity of attending a locomotive in steam or a traction-engine rally. Now the others were carried along by his enthusiasm. It was agreed that they would all work next day on restoring the Bowdler's Apollo.

'I might have to go into Westover first,' Helen predicted; 'but I'll come and help as soon as I get back. You must keep out of sight of the men, and time their coming and going so that we know when it will be best to use the traction engine.'

'Ahem! I've thought of a riddle,' Robin announced.

'What is it?'

'When is a dog no good as a messenger?'

'That's easy,' said Peg, who knew the way her brother's mind worked.

'What's the answer, then?' her cousins demanded.

'It's when he has lost his bark.'

☆ ☆ ☆

Before she went to bed that night Helen again consulted the big dictionary in the sitting-room.

She looked for *narrow* and *narrowing* without discovering anything that would throw light on what had been overheard in the Treacle Mine. Then she looked for *nerrowing, nerrowin* and *neroin,* but could find nothing. She thought of *heroin* and read:

> HEROIN, a concentrated narcotic drug prepared from morphine, administered to alleviate pain, but addictive and used illegally to induce a false sense of well-being (from Greek 'Eros, a hero, one who does superhuman deeds).

One word led to another. She looked up *narcotic* and found it meant causing drowsiness or stupor or insensibility. Then she looked up *morphine,* and found it was an alkaloid prepared from opium. When she looked up *alkaloid* she found it could be 'any one of a large number of nitrogenous vegetable drugs'.

104

Helen knew that *addictive* referred to a habit that was difficult to break. The words were rather confusing and did not seem to be getting her very far in her quest. It was all too complicated.

She stifled a yawn. She wanted to be a journalist, Helen reminded herself, which involved finding things out; but she must not let looking up words become addictive! She closed the dictionary and made for bed, but the unexplained *narrowing* or *nerrowing* still bothered her.

14

Bowdler's Apollo

Christopher Bairstow usually went to market once a week, either to Market Lydford on Tuesday or Westover on Thursday. Even if he had no livestock to sell or buy, he liked to think that such excursions beyond the farm gate kept him in touch with market trends and farming fashions. In fact, he enjoyed seeing his friends and meeting business acquaintances.

Danny had worked all day this Wednesday with his usual vigour and cheerfulness, so when he arrived as usual at milking time on Thursday morning Christopher dismissed any fears he had had that Danny might have been incubating an infectious disease. Market Lydford had been out of the question on Tuesday morning because of Danny's strange behaviour, so now the Thursday market at Westover was Christopher's only choice for his weekly excursion.

Helen seized the opportunity of a lift to Westover. Adrian asked her, 'Will you get something for me? I'll write down exactly what to ask for.'

'I'm coming too,' their mother said. 'I have shopping to do. We can all get back here for a late lunch about one or half past.'

☆ ☆ ☆

When Peg and the two boys set off for the Apollo traction

engine they were heavily laden. Adrian and Robin had made their selection of tools from the farm workshop; Adrian knew his father would not mind, provided everything was returned safely. They did not want to interrupt their work once they had started on the traction engine, so it is not surprising that they tended to over-cater. There were large and small spanners, an adjustable wrench, several screwdrivers, pliers, a hacksaw with some spare blades, various files, a hammer, a long-spouted oil can, a quart of lubricating oil, a can of penetrating fluid, a tin of grease, another of joint compound, sheets of emery paper, a discarded toothbrush, old newspapers, some worn-out shirts torn up for wipers, Adrian's copper pipes and brass fittings, and a tin of metal polish that Peg added at the last moment. Some of this gear was contained in two sacks that Peg tied together and slung across the front of her saddle, having first shown them to Pippin and rattled them so that the pony would not be scared. The rest was carried in Adrian's leather satchel on his crossbar or slung about their persons.

Besides the tools, Peg brought Adrian's field glasses. One of her jobs today was to act as lookout and warn the boys to hide if she spotted the vintage Perugi. It would be disastrous if the tall man came down to the timber yard to find out what they were doing. Her other task was to start collecting firewood.

The thief who had stolen the copper pipes from the traction engine might have wrenched them off with the aid of the fire irons as levers; if he had had proper tools he would very likely have unscrewed all the brass fittings and taken off the heavy brass name-plate as well, to sell as scrap metal. Fortunately the sight glass of the water gauge was not smashed.

With spanners, Robin and Adrian now undid the gland nuts of the compression fittings that had held the copper pipes. It was something of a struggle to get the broken stubs free, but with the use of the wrench and some tapping with a heavy spanner head they managed to get the gland rings off, one fitting after another.

Robin instructed Adrian how the new pipes should run; Adrian selected pieces of copper tube with more or less suitable bends, cut them to length with the hacksaw, smoothed the ends with a file and emery paper, and offered them to the now vacant sockets. To the boys' relief, all was right for size, and with the help of what Robin called 'gentle persuasion' they manipulated the gland fittings on to each copper pipe, painted the joints with sealing compound and screwed them up very tight – all except two, whose gland rings were too distorted to use again. Robin frowned.

'Don't worry,' said Adrian. 'Helen's buying me some spare rings in Westover.'

Next the boys busied themselves with getting moving parts working freely. The traction engine seemed to have been well greased when it was last used, so penetrating fluid and lubricating oil worked wonders in easing stiff bearings.

Peg meanwhile was equally busy. Dry sticks would be needed for lighting the boiler fire, and logs would be needed for burning to raise steam. There were plenty of dry sticks; Peg built a pile of them, just under the roof of the shed in case of rain. Then she started collecting logs.

Besides the timber that had been squared into fencing posts, rails and planks, Peg found there were logs of two sorts. There were round, regular-sized pieces like pit-props, neatly cut and stacked at one end of the shed. She assumed that these had been prepared for some purpose and might one day be fetched away. But there were also rough offcuts, sawn or axed from limbs of trees that had been felled. These were of various sizes, some too big for her to handle, others that she could manage, and these she decided were free for anyone. 'It's like gleaning,' she told herself as she steadily fetched and piled them near the Apollo.

By lunch-time all three were well pleased with their

morning's work and felt encouraged to go on with what they had planned.

'What about water?' Peg asked.

'There is some water in the boiler,' Robin told her, 'but more will be needed. It's a chicken-and-egg situation. You can't suck up water until you've raised steam, and you can't raise steam until you've got water in the boiler. What we've got to do is make sure the water tank at the rear is full. I've measured the tank by eye; it's about thirty-six cubic feet, so I reckon it holds about two hundred and twenty-five gallons – something like a hundred and fifty buckets, you might say – and we'll have to fetch it all from the pond by hand.'

They collected the tools and returned to Up-hill Farm for lunch.

Helen was back. 'I've spent the whole morning in the Central Reference Library,' she told them. 'I looked through all the encyclopaedias to see if there was anything that sounded like *nerrowing,* but there wasn't. Then I started on the shelves of technical books; there were all sorts. I was on the point of giving up, because it was nearly time to meet Daddy at the car park. But then I found a big book called *Klein's Dictionary of Applied Chemistry,* and there was what I was looking for. I'll tell you about it in the barn tonight.'

Before they all set out for the traction engine that afternoon, Helen collected two buckets from the stable and Adrian borrowed one from the cowshed and one from the wash-house. The boys' first task now was to complete the pipe jointing, using the gland rings that Helen had brought.

Just down the slope beyond the timber yard was a dew-pond. This was probably the reason for siting the timber yard there, so that a steam traction engine used for working the saw bench could draw its water by suction. Although the pond was near, filling the Apollo's water tank by bucket now proved to be a gruelling chore. Adrian stood with his wellington boots actually in the pond; Peg staggered up and down a short stretch of sloping bank; Helen spanned a wide gap on the level, in the middle of the human chain, and Robin was perched on the traction engine to lift the buckets and empty them into the tank.

Filling the water tank was not without incident. They had scarcely started when Peg called Adrian's attention to a bog-bean in flower, growing in the dew-pond. Adrian, anxious to see it closer, ventured too far into the pond and let one of his wellington boots fill with water. Unthinkingly, instead of coming straight out on to dry land, he tried to stand on one leg while he pulled the boot off and emptied it. The result of this manoeuvre was that the other boot sank deep into ooze and filled with water, so that when he tried to lift that foot he found it was heavily weighted and held down by suction. Robin, gesticulating wildly on the traction engine, shouted instructions to Adrian what to do to extricate himself, but in so doing he let his attention wander from guiding buckets into the tank; the next bucketful missed the hopper and poured over Helen.

Humping buckets of water took a very long time, but at last Robin declared there was sufficient.

Then all four concentrated on fuel for the morrow. Peg was congratulated on her morning's achievement. There was some discussion on how crumpled newspaper, sticks and chumps of wood should be laid so that flames would leap along the fire box when a match was applied through the fire door, but finally all was arranged to Robin's satisfaction and the footplate was stacked with more chumps to be thrust in as soon as the fire was well alight.

There was scarcely room for four people on the footplate at once, so Peg busied herself with a piece of rag and the tin of metal polish. The great Joseph Bowdler himself could scarcely have been prouder than Peg when she stepped back to admire the brightly polished brass name-plate:

APOLLO:
Jos. Bowdler,
Engineer,
N'hampton

Giving a final shine to the copper pipes, Peg remembered her responsibility as lookout. She picked up the field glasses and surveyed the track stretching from the foot of the Bradbury Castle bridle path to the quarry fence. It was well that she did so.

Three times previously that day she had seen the Perugi. It was no longer drawing the horse trailer. Soon after she and the boys had arrived at the timber yard that morning they had watched from behind drifts of willow-herb as the Perugi came from the Westover direction with the two men in it; the shorter man had got out and unlocked the gate, padlocking it again from inside after his companion had driven through. Then the watchers heard the car complete the short distance to the Treacle Mine entrance. About twelve o'clock Peg had caught the sound of the motor again, and the three hid and watched while the Perugi and the tall man alone emerged through the gate and sped away westward. Some two hours later the car returned with the tall man and disappeared once more behind the gate and fence.

'I guess he's had a good lunch at a pub and brought back some sandwiches for his buddy,' Robin had suggested.

Now the four hid and watched as the Perugi emerged from the quarry. The tall man got out each time to open and shut the gate, and as he drove off the watchers could see he was alone.

'What's happened to Humpty-Dumpty?' inquired Adrian.

'He's working overtime,' laughed Robin. 'His mate's burnt the treacle and he's having to stay behind to clear up the mess.'

'The Perugi will be coming back,' Adrian warned. 'We've half an hour to get clear. Come on.'

111

They quickly gathered up the buckets and what remained of all they had brought that morning, and made for home as fast as they could. It was a relief to reach the metalled road and turn down to Up-hill Farm without meeting the Perugi and its driver.

The evening turned out to be a wet one. The four decided they were too tired for talking in the barn and voted for an early night, in anticipation of much to be done next day.

Peg wanted to take a last peep at the kittens before turning in. She climbed the stone steps at the end of the stable and found Esmeralda reclining on a pile of sacks, fondly licking her four offspring. Peg could not resist the urge to pick up and fondle each kitten in turn, but under the last one, the tortoiseshell, she was surprised to find a white postcard. It had not been there before. Had someone written a card of congratulation for Esmeralda, just for fun?

Peg picked it up, turned it over and read the scrawled block letters:

BEWARE OF RADIOACTIVITY.
YOU HAVE BEEN WARNED!

15

Open, Sesame

There was heavy rain during the night, but Friday morning started fine. The weather forecaster had announced high pressure over Ireland and a deep depression moving eastward across southern England; he predicted more rain to come.

At Up-hill Farm, Christopher put his head in at the back door to say that Danny had not turned up for work. 'I may be a little late for breakfast,' he said.

'I was going to do some work in the flower garden this morning,' Mary replied, 'but the weather's not very promising. I'll come and give you a hand instead. The children can get their own breakfasts.'

In fact this suited 'the children' very well. Adrian was out early, before other members of the household, to go and light the fire in the Apollo. At the farm, Robin cooked himself an early breakfast and sped out to the timber yard to take over the Apollo so that Adrian could come back for breakfast. By seven-thirty Helen and Peg had eggs, bacon and toast ready, and called to Christopher and Mary that they could come in for breakfast as soon as they were free.

Mary remarked how enjoyable it was to eat a good meal that she had not had to cook herself. It was an added bonus when she found three volunteers ready to clear away the breakfast things and do the washing-up. She did not know that this was part of a pre-arranged time-table.

Out at the timber yard, Robin stowed Helen's bicycle behind a stack of logs under the open shed. The wind was blowing from the north, and high banks of anvil-shaped cloud were piling up to the west, but he was prepared for wet weather, and was wearing wellington boots and a waterproof coat with a hood that could be turned up if needed. He knew that it would take at least four hours to raise steam, but besides adjusting the dampers and feeding the fire box with wood there were things to do while he was waiting.

In case of any unwanted collection of water in the cylinders during starting-up, Robin first made sure that the cylinder relief taps were open. Then he tried the movement of the reversing lever and found it all right. He checked the engagement of the winding drum, which would wind in the cable and chain pulling the oak tree, but there was no steam yet to try it out. The wheels of the traction engine were chocked with split logs, and he spun the handwheel of the rear wheel brake to make sure, first, that the brake could be released and second that it could be applied when needed.

When the Perugi appeared from the Westover direction about nine o'clock he crouched low until it had passed through the quarry gate. It was without the horse trailer, and the hood had been raised to protect the two occupants from rain. Robin hoped they had not noticed the smoke rising from the Apollo's smoke stack, or at least attached no importance to it. He knew that Helen, Peg and Adrian would not arrive until nine-thirty, by which time it was calculated the coast would be clear.

Robin tried the injector, but was not surprised to find there was not enough steam pressure as yet to suck water, so he busied himself feeding wood into the fire box and piling the footplate with more chumps from ground level.

The wind had backed to north-west and rain was falling intermittently when the three others arrived, accompanied by Shep. Adrian stowed his bike as Robin had

114

done. Peg and Helen tethered their ponies at the end of the shed so that they could browse in the open air or move into shelter if the rain became heavy.

Adrian helped Robin to load the heavy lumber chains and shackles on to the rear of the Apollo. Helen heaved more chumps on to the footplate.

Robin tried the injector again, and finding enough steam proudly demonstrated to the others the rise of water level in the sight glass. Encouraged by this he opened the steam regulator valve, expecting to see the flywheel turn. Nothing happened.

By this time steam was beginning to blow off from the safety valve. The boiler fire was burning fiercely, so Robin decided it was time to reduce the draught to the fire box, which he did. Now he opened the regulator valve again. Nothing happened. He opened it wider. Still nothing happened. This was disconcerting. Had he done something wrong? Or left something undone? He tried starting the flywheel by hand, first one way, then the other, but it would not budge. He felt a flash of panic when he reflected that an irresistible force against an immovable mass could only result in an explosion, and he looked imploringly at Adrian, standing beside him, whose smiling face gave no indication that he was aware of the crisis Robin was facing. His own face had somehow acquired some streaks of soot.

The panic was only momentary, for Robin belatedly remembered reading in one of his books that a compound-cylinder engine will not start if its high-pressure crank happens to have stopped in the dead centre position. The remedy, he fortunately recalled, was to joggle a spring-loaded rod that would operate a valve to let steam into the low-pressure cylinder, whose piston, being at mid-stroke, should move at once. Robin had noticed the rod earlier without recognizing its purpose. He did not know if it should be pushed or pulled, but moving it against the spring at once had the desired effect. As if with a sigh of relief the working mechanism started to move; there was a

115

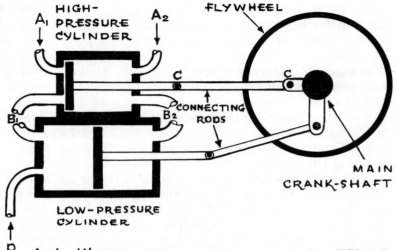

HIGH-PRESSURE CYLINDER A_1 A_2 FLYWHEEL

C C

CONNECTING RODS

B_1 B_2

MAIN CRANK-SHAFT

LOW-PRESSURE CYLINDER

D

A_1, A_2. WHEN THE REGULATOR VALVE IS OPENED, STEAM IS ADMITTED BY VALVE GEAR TO ALTERNATE ENDS OF THE HIGH-PRESSURE CYLINDER.

B_1, B_2. CONTROLLED BY VALVE GEAR (NOT SHOWN) STEAM IS PASSED ON TO THE LOW-PRESSURE CYLINDER.

C-C. THE HIGH-PRESSURE CONNECTING ROD HAS STOPPED IN A DEAD CENTRAL POSITION, SO CANNOT MOVE UNTIL —

D, LIVE STEAM IS ADMITTED DIRECT TO THE LOW-PRESSURE CYLINDER BY OPENING THE SPECIAL VALVE FOR THAT PURPOSE.

Later, back at the farm house, Robin borrowed Adrian's ruler and compass to draw this diagram, which explains why the flywheel would not start to turn when he expected it to.

rush of steam; the flywheel turned and gathered speed.

Robin mopped his brow and pretended the beads of sweat thereon were due to the heat from the boiler fire. He adjusted the regulator to his satisfaction and listened to the rhythmic throb of the pistons. He closed the cylinder relief taps, which had been spurting thin jets of steam.

Adrian glanced at his watch. 'We've thirty minutes left for getting clear of the quarry,' he told Robin. 'We must get along to the stag-headed oak before the Perugi reappears. Can we go?'

Getting the traction engine ready and raising steam had been slow work. Now events happened in quick succession.

Helen and Peg rejoined the ponies and held their bridles in case they were frightened by the traction engine when it started moving. Adrian removed the split logs that were chocking the engine wheels, then climbed up to the footplate, there to help Robin stoke up the fire once more before steaming away. Standing behind the steering wheel, Robin signalled to him to spin the handwheel that released the rear wheel brake, while he himself engaged forward gear and opened the regulator valve wide, giving the heavy traction engine sufficient steam to get under way and climb the rough slope from the timber yard to the main track along the hillside.

The Apollo responded nobly and chugged up the incline with no difficulty. Shep raced alongside, barking excitedly. Peg and Helen waved and cheered.

As the traction engine reached level ground its speed increased. The boys intended to turn right at the top of the rise and proceed along the main track towards the stag-headed oak as quickly as possible. The turn would have been a sharp one at any speed, and now the Apollo was moving fast. Adrian suddenly remembered his father's advice about driving the farm tractor: 'Don't let it run away with you.' But now it was Robin who was working the steering chains and controlling the regulator. These needed skills that Robin had not acquired.

The Apollo raced on towards the quarry, just missed the newly painted notice board, and like a battering ram crashed into the corrugated-iron fence. Fence posts and rails snapped like matchsticks before this onslaught, and the traction engine's heavy wheels rolled over the thin corrugated metal with a noise like thunder.

Robin frantically shut the regulator valve; Adrian spun the handle of the rear wheel brake. Slowed by the roughness of the quarry floor, the Apollo came to a halt.

Within the same minute a pair of hands had unlocked the chain that secured the quarry gate. There by the opened gateway were the black Perugi and its dark, tall driver. This was earlier than the boys had expected, but everything had suddenly gone so badly wrong it no longer seemed to matter.

Helen and Peg had watched the career of the Apollo; now they came galloping on the ponies to find out what was going on.

Then all present became aware of somebody else who had arrived on the scene, wheeling a heavy bicycle. He had a rosy weather-beaten face, a long straight nose, crisp grey hair, a neat moustache, and dark eyes that flashed penetratingly from beneath bushy eyebrows. He wore a deerstalker hat, a green raincoat, knickerbocker trousers, woollen stockings, and brown boots that shone with much polishing. It could be none other than Lieutenant-Colonel John Henry Irving Savage, DSO, of Walden Lodge.

16

The cloudburst

Alarmed though he must have been by the havoc caused by the Apollo, the Colonel's first words were directed at the tall man beside the Perugi.

'Gerry, what are you doing here on my estate? I told you I never want to see you again.'

'It's all right, Uncle. I've come back to retrieve your fortune.'

'Nonsense!'

'I've always felt sorry about what happened. It was sheer bad luck. But now I've found a way to put everything right.'

'I don't believe you.'

'Do you see that notice? I'm prospecting for uranium. It's radioactive, you know. There's a lot of it in this hill. There's gold and silver too.'

Gerontius d'Arcy was letting his eloquence carry him away from truth. It had happened before, to his undoing, in the promotion of worthless investments. The Colonel would have none of it.

'The Romans worked out all the worthwhile ores in these hills many hundred years ago.'

'Ah, but they didn't have modern technology. With new skills we can detect and analyse where they never could. Take cadmium, for instance; I don't suppose the Romans even knew of its existence. These hills are full of cadmium ore. I have a very clever chemist friend who is working with

119

me to locate and assess rich veins.'

'You found rich veins on this estate once before – and bled me white.'

'Oh, but this is different.'

D'Arcy lit a fresh cigarette from the stub of the one he was smoking. Helen noticed that his fingers were stained brown with nicotine.

The wrangle between step-uncle and step-nephew might have gone on indefinitely, but from the dark sky there suddenly came a flash of lightning followed immediately by a loud clap of thunder; rain and hail began to fall heavily.

Gerontius d'Arcy opened the door of his car and got into the driver's seat as if to take shelter from the storm. The Colonel moved to the other side, intending to occupy the passenger seat and go on talking. But d'Arcy did not open the near-side door. Instead he slammed his own door shut, started the engine, and before anyone could stop him drove the car out of the quarry and along the green track in the direction of the cross lane and Westover. Water flew up as he charged furiously through puddles, and before he disappeared into the distance it was apparent to the watchers that the track was already very wet and the powerful Perugi was skidding from side to side as its driver sought to avoid irregularities at speed.

At the onset of the downpour Adrian pulled his hood well over his head and made for the tunnel entrance. He was followed quickly by Helen and Peg with Shep and the ponies, which had been a little startled by the noise of the storm. Robin, who had tried to shelter under the traction engine, presently ran across to join them. The Colonel picked up his bicycle and did likewise. All crowded into the tunnel mouth.

There was another brilliant flash of lightning, thunder rolled, and the torrential downpour seemed to double in intensity. Conversation was difficult under these conditions, and for a few minutes nobody spoke.

The Colonel looked at the two boys. Then, 'What the

120

devil do you mean by driving my traction engine?' he demanded fiercely.

This was a difficult question to answer in a few words, and the boys scarcely knew where to begin.

Helen came to the rescue. 'You must be Colonel Savage,' she said. 'I am Helen Bairstow; you know my father. This is my brother Adrian, and these are our cousins Robin and Margaret Gaskell. We borrowed your traction engine for a very good reason: to gain entry to the Treacle Mine to collect evidence about what is going on here – illegally, so we believe.'

'You have certainly smashed your way in, so far. You have probably smashed the traction engine too.'

'No, sir,' interposed Robin. Raindrops trickled vertically down his face, crossing the horizontal streaks of soot and making a grotesque chequerboard pattern. 'I have looked everything over, so far as the rain would allow, and there is nothing broken.'

'We replaced all the copper pipes that had been torn out by thieves,' Peg chimed in, 'but we don't intend to charge you for materials and labour.'

It is probable that the Colonel already knew the copper pipes had been stolen, so their replacement now softened his attitude. He even seemed to be amused by Peg's last words; his mood changed and he looked a little less fierce.

'We wanted to move a fallen oak tree,' Adrian hastened to explain; 'it had blocked the other entrance to the Treacle Mine. Robin and I went down the Swallock once to find out what the men were doing and why fish in Bincombe Pool were poisoned. But we decided it was too dangerous to go down the Swallock again, and we needed to find out more and to let the girls see, so that they could ...' Adrian searched for the right word. 'So that they could corroborate our evidence in court.'

Any detailed explanation that might have followed was cut short by the arrival of a blue four-wheel-drive Field Ranger. Falling raindrops bounced like silver stars on its

121

bonnet. The driver, a big man in a raincoat, clutching a battery lantern in one hand, swung down from the cab and made a dash through the rain for the tunnel entrance.

'What a day!' he greeted the group already sheltering there. They responded appropriately. Then, 'Will you please let me pass?' he asked. 'I want to go into the Treacle Mine.'

The Colonel barred his way. 'Who are you and what are you doing here?' he demanded.

'My name is Coleman. I am a waterworks chemist, and I am making an investigation.'

'I suppose you chemists can find minerals where the Romans never dreamed of looking.'

Derek Coleman hesitated before replying to what appeared to be a strange question – if it was a question at all. Then it flashed through his mind that the old gentleman might be an archaeologist or other genuine seeker of information, so he said, 'Well, yes. With modern technology we can detect and analyse where the ancients never could.'

This sounded so much like what the Colonel had heard previously that it seemed to confirm his suspicion that the newcomer was the 'very clever chemist friend' of his worthless nephew.

The Colonel said, with a hint of sarcasm in his voice, 'Doesn't it occur to you to seek permission to enter on private property before you start your pursuits?'

'I never exceed my lawful powers, sir. But this is a case of some urgency.'

'Well, I am the owner of this estate, and you seem to be doing things around what we call the Treacle Mine without asking my permission – a permission I may not be willing to give.'

'Then you must be Colonel Savage, sir. Please may I have your permission to enter the mine? I am looking for the source of some water pollution. It may be of serious public importance.'

'I have been given to understand that you are searching

122

for minerals.'

'That is the remarkable thing and why I am here now. The samples I have had are quite free of mineral contaminants – salts of lead or cadmium, for instance –and what I am looking for is an organic source.'

Peg looked imploringly at Adrian as if to tell him it was time he said something to resolve the Colonel's and the Chief Chemist's cross-purposes. Adrian might have done so, but the curious conversation was interrupted by yet another arrival: a smart silver-grey car and its driver.

17

Doctor Hobday

The surgery session at Beech House this Friday morning
was something like the previous Tuesday's. The waiting-
room was full and noisy again.

Doctor Hobday's first patient was Danny. None of his
shirt buttons and few of any others were done up. His dark
curly hair looked like that of an Old English sheep dog.

' 'Ullo, Doctor,' Danny said. 'Look, I do feel queer. Can
you give I some tablets?'

The Doctor started to ask questions, then took down
from the wall a large-scale map of Bincombe mounted on
cardboard.

'Number Twenty in the High Street, isn't it?' he
inquired. From a tray on his desk he took a glass-headed
pin and stuck it into the map to represent No 20, High
Street, Bincombe. From a drawer in his desk he drew out a
big sheet of writing paper ruled with horizontal lines in
blue and vertical columns in red. He wrote Danny's name
at the top of the left-hand column.

Then the Doctor made a routine examination of Danny
and asked more questions, but as he proceeded he marked
the columns of his sheet of paper with ticks and
crosses.

'You tell me you felt bad on Tuesday morning, just as
you do now. How did the feeling come on – on Tuesday,
that is?'

Danny answered this and more questions.

'So you felt all right when you got up, but when you had had two cups of tea with milk and sugar you started to feel dreamy, as if your body didn't belong to you.'

'That's right.'

'Are you sure you didn't put any whisky or brandy in your tea?'

Danny shook his head.

'And you didn't have a drink of beer or scrumpy, or anything like that, before you set out for Up-hill Farm?'

Danny shook his head again.

'Did you have anything to eat – anything at all besides your two cups of tea?'

Danny looked at the Doctor as if he thought he was being tiresome.

'All right, I just want to be sure. Now, this morning, did you do and feel exactly as you did on Tuesday?'

'No, Doctor.'

'What was different, then?'

'I come along to you.'

Doctor Hobday looked up from his ticks and crosses. 'Where does your wife buy her tea?' he asked.

'Post Office Stores, yer in Bincombe.'

'Where does she buy her sugar?'

'Same place, I s'pose.'

'And you have milk from the farm – Mr Bairstow's?'

'Yes.'

'Do you know if any of the Bairstow family have been off-colour or what you might call queer – lately, I mean?'

Danny shook his head once more. 'They can all be queer at times, in their diff'rent ways, but not in the sorta way you means, Doctor.'

'Is your cottage on the water main?'

'Yes.'

Then the 'phone rang: a secretary at the Public Health Laboratory telephoned to say that no obvious disease germs had been detected in the swabs taken by Doctor Hobday on Tuesday; further tests were being made, and a full report would follow later.

125

The Doctor turned back to Danny. 'Well, that's about all, thank you.'

'What about they tablets?'

The Doctor thought for a moment. Then he stood up and fetched a wide-mouthed amber jar from a cupboard. It was labelled in his own tiny, almost unreadable script *Un. plac.*, which he alone knew stood for 'Universal placebo', meaning something to be handed out when patients expected it but nothing was really needed. He solemnly counted out sixteen white tablets and put them into a small envelope. There was just room on it to write Danny's name, the date and the words 'Take two tablets with water every four hours'.

'You'd better go home for the rest of the morning. You can take two of these as soon as you get there,' the Doctor said. 'Have a strong cup of coffee – but no alcohol. You'll be all right again very soon.'

'Ta,' said Danny, and went out through the noisy waiting-room.

Patients followed one another into and out of the consulting-room. Charley Barley was the sixth to be seen. He was the greatest source of noise, for he seemed to be in bad humour and was complaining loudly about everything, not least the magazines provided for the patients to look at while waiting.

'All them magazines is last year's,' he stormed. 'An' what proper man wants t'read *Lady's Own*? 'Tisn't decent. *Man's Own* is what I wants, an' lots o' nice pitchers, not silly ol' knittin' patterns.'

Doctor Hobday smiled. He would have liked to tease Charley Barley about the sort of pictures he wanted; instead he said soothingly, 'I didn't expect to see you again so soon. What's the trouble?'

'What's the trouble?' Charley repeated. 'It's me arthuritis, o' course. After I leave yer on Tuesday it come on bad.'

The Doctor asked a few questions. Then: 'Did you have your three cuppas this morning?'

126

'No, come t'think of it I didn't have but one.'

The Doctor stuck another pin into the map and added a line of ticks and crosses to the big sheet of paper. Satisfied that, whatever Charley's condition on Tuesday, it was arthritis that now afflicted him, the Doctor wrote a prescription.

'The chemist will give you some tablets,' he said. 'Take one three times a day with your food. Ask the next patient to come in, please.'

The next patient was Alfreda, and it was at once apparent that she was pixillated again.

'*Dear* Doctor Hobday,' she began, and advanced unsteadily as if to embrace him; but as she did so one of her feet met the corner of a weighing machine that stood against the wall, and she stumbled forward. At the same moment Doctor Hobday got up from his chair, intending to place himself at the far end of the room; but time was not on his side. To save herself from falling, Alfreda flung her arms around his neck.

'*Atchully,*' she said dreamily, 'that's the second time I've been swept off my feet this morning. The first time it was the postman that drives the mail van. "Drinking again on duty, Miss Jones," he said. *Reelly,* what could he have been thinking? Oh, Doctor, after I left you on Tuesday I *laid* down and drifted right off to sleep. But when I woke up it was dark and I felt *dreadful.* I just laid there until it was light. Then I heard my brother moving, because he gets up ever so early. I wanted him to give you a ring, but he said no. "Elfie," he said, "that dear man needs all the sleep he can get. Don't you disturb him." '

She prattled on, but Doctor Hobday interrupted. 'Has your brother been – er – pixillated, either on Tuesday or this morning?'

'No, he's never ill reelly.'

'Does he have an early-morning cup or cups of tea?'

'Oh no. Atchully he's quite busy and doesn't have anything until breakfast-time, and then he has a proper breakfast, eggs and bacon and coffee and toast and marmalade.'

'Do you know where he buys the tea he sells in the Post Office Stores?'

'From the wholesalers in Westover.'

'And sugar?'

'From the wholesalers.'

Doctor Hobday tried to be as businesslike with Alfreda as she normally was with him over the Post Office counter. He put ticks and crosses on his sheet of paper, and continued to do so as he asked a few more questions. Finally he stuck another pin in the map.

'Miss Jones, you seem to be suffering from something that has affected other people in the village. My advice to you is to go home and make yourself a reelly . . .' He hesitated. '. . . A really strong cup of coffee. You can go on working if you feel like it. If you don't feel like work, go for a brisk walk in the fresh air.'

He looked out of the window and saw that rain was starting to fall.

'I'm sure the weather will clear up again soon,' he added hopefully, and keeping well behind the door he opened it for her to leave him.

By the time all the patients had been seen the pins stuck in the map formed a cluster around Bincombe High Street, and the lines on the big sheet of paper were filled in down to the bottom with names, ticks, crosses and a few question marks.

It had been the longest surgery session he could remember. He looked at his watch, then picked up the telephone and dialled the Walden Water Board offices in Westover.

'Hello. This is Doctor Hobday. Please put me through to your Chief Chemist. . . . Well, may I speak to his deputy?'

There was a pause, then he heard a woman's voice say, 'Assistant Chemist. Can I help you?'

'Good morning. Doctor Hobday speaking. I wanted to ask your Chief Chemist if you've had any trouble lately with drinking water at Bincombe.'

'No trouble with the drinking water there. At least, not to my knowledge, and I should know because I do the analyses.'

'You sound a little uncertain.'

'Well, we have had two samples of water from a fish pond there. In fact our Chief Chemist is out at Bincombe now. He should be back here by this afternoon, but you might catch him at the Meter House or perhaps somewhere round Bradbury Castle. He's driving a blue Field Ranger.'

'Thank you very much. I think I will try to find him.'

Doctor Hobday looked at his watch again and out of the window. Rain was still falling. Then, folding the big sheet of paper and putting it into an inside breast pocket, he walked through into his house for a cup of coffee before donning rain wear and setting out to find the Chief Chemist. As he went out, Anthracite sneaked in, looking very wet.

First the Doctor drove down to Bincombe Pool, and turning up his raincoat collar he got out of the car to look closely at the water there. It looked cloudy; raindrops made many circles on the surface, but through the thin curtain of falling rain he could see a few trout lying without movement, more or less on their sides, their pale bellies showing.

Next he motored up to the Meter House. He got out of the car again and tried the Meter House door; it was locked, and there was no sign of the Chief Chemist or of his blue Field Ranger.

As the Doctor returned to his car the hovering storm broke in fury. Lightning flashed, thunder cracked and rolled. First there was a deluge of large raindrops, then a fusillade of hail stones. For a minute Doctor Hobday could scarcely see through his windscreen. In spite of the weather he decided to carry on up the hill and take the green track that led in the direction of Bradbury Castle, so he sat and waited, hoping the worst of the storm would quickly pass.

Tired of waiting, the Doctor restarted his engine and motored slowly past Up-hill Farm. Heavy rain continued to lash his windows and drummed on roof and bonnet. The gutters on each side of the lane had become rushing stream beds carrying weeds, earth and stones. As he reached the top of the rise and was about to turn into the track on his left he was startled by a large black sports car that shot out from the gloom, lurched round dangerously in front of him, raking his near side with a wave of muddy water and gravel, and careered down the lane towards the main road.

Doctor Hobday proceeded cautiously along the glade, now intersected by torrents of surface water. When he reached the Bradbury Castle fork he recognized that it was no more than a bridle path and quite impassable for an ordinary motor car in wet weather. He continued on, and presently through the rain made out a blue motor vehicle parked in a disused quarry near a steam traction engine.

18

Occupied territory

Arrived at the old quarry, Doctor Hobday drove through the open gateway and parked beside the blue Field Ranger. He turned up his collar again, opened the car door and made a rapid transfer to the shelter of the Treacle Mine entrance.

Recognition between Colonel Savage and the Doctor was mutual; they shook hands. Then the Doctor turned to the biggish man standing there. 'Are you the Water Board's Chief Chemist, may I ask? I am Doctor Hobday.'

'How d'you do? Yes, I am,' the Chief Chemist replied; 'Derek Coleman by name.' He added, 'I don't know who these young people are.'

It was Adrian who spoke. 'I am Adrian Bairstow, from Up-hill Farm. You spoke to me over the telephone.'

'Oh yes. That's how I come to be here. Have you discovered anything more?'

Adrian hesitated, again wondering how to begin.

'Quite a lot more, but not everything,' put in Helen, in her big-sisterly manner. 'I am Adrian's sister, and these are our cousins. Colonel Savage and Mr Coleman, you must listen to us. Adrian and Robin have been down into the Treacle Mine through the Swallock. There are two men making some sort of chemical in there, and we think some of their drainage polluted the fish pool. But we've got to find out more, and that's why we wanted to get inside the Treacle Mine from the other entrance.'

'I am interested too,' said Doctor Hobday. 'That's why I'm here.'

The Chief Chemist asked, 'Why is it called "the Treacle Mine"?' He addressed Colonel Savage. 'Is it only a joke?'

'People usually say it's just a joke,' the Colonel told him, 'but it must be a joke of very long standing, and I believe there is more to it than that. Estate documents in my possession show that the name "Trekel Mine" was in use two hundred and fifty years ago. It sounds as if it might originally have meant "Trickle Mine" because of trickling water; but scholars have suggested the name could be very old indeed and come from *triaquilum,* which is Latin, meaning a device with three eagles – perhaps the badge or standard of a Roman legion. My grandfather told me that there used to be an inn at Bincombe called "The Three Eagles", but it went out of business soon after the mine closed, because there were no longer enough customers.'

Doctor Hobday asked, 'Was the *triaquilum* idea sparked off by the name of the inn, or did the name of the inn come from the *triaquilum* theory?'

'I suspect the name of the inn came first, and the *triaquilum* idea followed. "Three Eagles" sounds to me like a coat of arms, probably of some noble land-owner, from which the inn took its name. My own family's coat of arms has no eagles, but there are many coats of arms with three eagles. As to Roman eagles, no, I should think Roman eagles are red herrings.'

They all laughed at the Colonel's little joke.

'Right, now!' the Colonel resumed. 'We will all go into the Treacle Mine.' He beamed at the assembled group, pleased to take charge of a situation that earlier seemed to be out of his control.

'Never try to advance,' he went on, 'unless you know what your objective is and until you have scouted the position. My objective is to find out what's going on in the Treacle Mine and to assert my authority as the land-

132

owner. I once explored all these mine workings when I was a schoolboy. I suppose I was lucky not to come to harm, but at least I know the lie of the land. There is a tunnel that leads from here to a large cave called the Roman Cavern. It's called "Roman" because a bronze Roman sword was found there in 1722 when the old mine was redeveloped. You can see the sword now in the Westover Museum. The tunnel is called the Western Adit to distinguish it from another one, called the Eastern Adit, that proceeds beyond the Roman Cavern and comes out half a mile farther on along the hillside.'

'That must be where the big oak tree has fallen,' Adrian confirmed.

'Very well, I intend to make a reconnaisance – what we used to call a *reccé*. I must ask the rest of you to wait here till I come back. Will someone please lend me a torch?'

The Chief Chemist offered his battery lantern, and the Colonel went forward along the Western Adit.

'I wish we'd brought some sandwiches,' sighed Robin, while they waited. 'I could do with one right now.'

'Is that your dog?' asked the Chief Chemist, tactfully trying to take Robin's mind off the subject of food.

They all looked at Shep, who, tired of wandering about, had settled down at Peg's feet. The collie raised his head and gave a short bark.

'Hush!' Helen cried; but it was unlikely that the bark would have reached the distant Cavern, and the Colonel made no mention of it when at last he returned.

'I am amazed!' the Colonel reported. 'It's a small chemical factory. There's even electric light. I saw one man working there, and I want to talk to him presently, but I would like your support.'

He turned to the Doctor and the Chief Chemist.

'You youngsters can come too,' he added, 'as you've done so much already. But you must keep well behind and keep your dog to heel. Remember we are infiltrating enemy-occupied territory.'

The Colonel led the way back along the tunnel. To

Adrian and Robin it was like the approach to the Roman Cavern from the other end, what the Colonel had called the Eastern Adit, especially as the tunnel led downwards; but there were fewer puddles and no stream running alongside.

As they proceeded and the distant roar of tumbling water reached their ears, they heard also an echoing sound of hammering, like someone knocking in nails. After a while they all saw a glow of yellow light in the distance. They switched off the torches and moved on cautiously. Then the Roman Cavern came into full view.

To the newcomers the array of pipes and chemical apparatus, silhouetted against stalactites and stalagmites that gleamed in the naked light of the electric-light bulbs, presented a fantastic sight such as they had never before seen or imagined.

Adrian and Robin sensed at once that something was different from their first visit. They soon recognized that there was more noise, a greater sound of rushing water. The stream pouring from the leat in the Eastern Adit was now a roaring torrent, overlapping its channel and enveloping the water wheel in clouds of spray. They noticed too that the lake had risen and was occupying a greater area of the bedrock floor.

'Hi, there!' shouted the Colonel.

The stout man in the soiled white warehouse coat jumped in surprise. The hammer he was using dropped from his hand.

'Hi, there!' the Colonel repeated, coming forward into the electric light. 'I want to talk to you.'

The stout man walked slowly backward alongside the wooden bench. He opened a drawer at the end and drew out a pistol.

'Get out of here!' he shouted defiantly, waving the pistol in the air.

The Colonel calmly ignored the threat and continued to move forward until he was fully lit by the glare of the electric-light bulbs. 'I want to talk to you,' he repeated. 'I am Colonel John Savage, the owner of this estate.'

The stout man retreated farther, now holding the pistol at waist level. Water was lapping round his feet like a rising tide.

'Drop that silly thing,' the Colonel shouted above the surrounding noise of water and apparatus. 'I want to know what you are doing here in the Treacle Mine.' He continued to advance.

The stout man had backed away until he reached the ramp that led up to the Eastern Adit. Water was now trickling down the stone steps, but he moved slowly up them, one at a time, until he reached the top, where being farther from the lights he was not so well illuminated. Then he dodged to one side, and in a moment was lost from view in the black shadows of the tunnel.

Suddenly there was a flash of fire from the darkness. A bullet whistled past the Colonel's head. Instinctively the old campaigner flung himself flat on the ground and wriggled into the shelter of the heap of Swedish turnips. The others quickly followed his example.

The report of the shot echoed and re-echoed around the Roman Cavern; above the noise of rushing water the echoes were answered by a distant vibration in the Western Adit, a muffled rumbling that continued for perhaps ten seconds.

To Shep the shot was like a starting pistol. He dashed from behind Peg, and barking loudly raced in a wide half-circle as if rounding up sheep. Veering past the water wheel, he bounded up the stone steps towards the darkness of the Eastern Adit.

The mouth of the tunnel was too dark for the onlookers to see exactly what happened next; they heard an angry bark, but could not be sure whether the stout man raised his leg to kick the collie or merely to ward him off. It was an unwise move, for as he raised his foot his other foot slipped on the wet rock. He flung up his arms to recover his balance, failed to do so and fell into the surging mill head. The fast-flowing stream carried him right over the turning water wheel and dropped him into the foaming mill tail, from which he was quickly swept into the lake.

To the watchers the man appeared to be either unconscious or no swimmer, for he made no effort to reach the shelving lake shore but allowed himself to be propelled into deep water swirling to dark recesses on the far side.

Helen was the nearest person to him. Without hesitation she flung off her raincoat and waded into the lake. Soon she too was caught in the current and was out of her depth, but with a few strokes she caught up with the floating man, seized him by the shoulders, and swimming on her back at a right angle to the current struggled to bring him to the lakeside, where ready hands helped them ashore.

The level of the lake was still rising, and even as Doctor Hobday checked that the man was not injured, and while Helen tried to wring water out of her clothes, the party was forced to retreat up the sloping floor.

The electric generator, driven by the water wheel under an excessive head of water, had been turning at high speed, and the electric lamps had been glowing brightly; but as the lake rose so did the tail water, the wheel turned more slowly and the lights gradually began to dim. Water started to mount the generator base, then its casing. There were blue sparks, mere flickers at first but increasing to brilliant flashes. Finally the generator was completely short-circuited; the lights all went out and there was total darkness.

What might then have been panic-stricken chaos became an orderly military withdrawal. The Colonel switched on his borrowed lantern and the two boys their torches, but the illumination was poor and local in comparison with the overhead electric lighting.

'When I give the order,' the Colonel said in a crisp voice, 'I want you to make your way back through the Western Adit. Boy One, in front there, is to lead the way with his torch. Doctor Hobday, you will accompany the Bairstow girl. Mr Coleman, you will march this man along with you.

136

The rest of you are to fall in behind. Boy Two, use your torch where needed and bring up the rear. Company, forward march!'

They moved off, up the uneven floor and into the Western Adit. The only noises now were the muffled pulsing at the foot of the water wheel and the rush of water pouring down the stone steps and over the wheel into the lake. These sounds faded as the Colonel's party picked its long way back to the outside world.

Halfway along the tunnel they came to a halt. There had been a roof fall. Now they knew the cause of the rumbling after the pistol shot.

The Colonel shone his lantern over the rubble. 'Here's a pretty mess,' was his comment; 'but we can't go back, so we will have to go forward. I will go ahead and explore; the rest of you must all keep well back. If I need any help to shift rocks I will flash my light twice, and Mr Coleman had better come then as he is the strongest. When I reach the far end of the rubble I will flash my lantern three times for the next comer. I want you to come through one at a time; we need not risk all being buried at once. You must keep your dog close at heel.'

Everyone looked round for Shep. Peg called. Adrian whistled. 'I saw him a little while ago,' he said.

'You must keep very quiet in case vibration brings more roof down,' the Colonel warned them. 'We were fortunate to come through earlier without trouble. Your collie must find his own way back. Now, I will advance and try to make sure all is safe. We will use the torches from both ends to light the way as well as we can.'

The Colonel went ahead, and after what seemed to be a long time those waiting saw three flashes from his lantern. Robin followed him. Helen went through next; although there were now torches shining from both ends of the roof fall she found that stumbling over rocks while encumbered by waterlogged garments was not easy. Doctor Hobday followed her. Then came the stout man; shocked by his immersion and weighed down by wet clothing, he had lost

137

his defiance and went through without causing trouble. He was closely followed by Derek Coleman.

'What have you got there?' Adrian asked Peg while holding the torch and waiting for the Chief Chemist to get clear.

Peg pressed a finger to her lips. 'It's the box the man was nailing up. Can you take it?'

'I've got something too. If I carry your box will you look after this for me? Don't unwrap it. Shep's had it in his mouth but it may still carry fingerprints.'

He took the box and handed Peg something wrapped in his handkerchief.

Adrian shone his torch to start Peg on her way, and he himself followed as soon as the flashing of the Colonel's lantern told him she was through the obstruction safely. The Colonel checked that all members of his party were now reassembled and continued to lead the way to the outside world. Shep had not reappeared.

When daylight became visible at the western end of the tunnel it was a misty grey light without sunshine, for the sky was overcast with heavy clouds and rain was still falling.

Once the bedraggled party reached the open air the stout man was placed in the front seat of the Field Ranger, like a prisoner between the tall frame of Colonel Savage and the bulky body of Derek Coleman at the steering wheel. Robin lifted the Colonel's bicycle into the back of the vehicle, Adrian stowed the wooden box and both boys climbed in.

'Would you please go down to the timber yard in front of you?' Adrian called out. 'We've left two bikes there.'

Meanwhile Doctor Hobday wrapped Helen in his car rug and placed her in his front passenger seat. He was about to start off, but Peg knocked on his window. He opened it.

'Doctor Hobday, could you please take this?' she asked. 'Adrian says don't unwrap it.'

It was the pistol. The Doctor took it and laid it in his glove tray.

'Peg,' said Helen, 'can you manage to bring Grimaldi back with you? You had better ride Pippin, as you are used to her, and lead Grimaldi, but don't let him try any tricks.'

The Doctor was about to start once more, when Shep reappeared. This was a relief for all.

Helen pointed to some tie-on labels lying in the Doctor's glove tray. 'Doctor Hobday, please may I have one of your labels?' she asked.

'They are all addressed to the Public Health Lab.,' he replied; then added, 'No, here's one that isn't. You can have that. What do you want it for?'

'I want to send a message, but I'll have to borrow something to write with.'

The Doctor offered his silver ball-point pen. Helen wrote, 'All safe. Home soon. Lots of soup for four extra, please.' She signed the message with a tiny outline of a harp.

Doctor Hobday noticed the logogram and asked, 'What's that for?'

'Can't you guess?'

'Oh, I see: Helen, Adrian, Robin and Peg. I must invent something like that for signing my prescriptions.'

Helen passed the label to Peg, who had come round to her window and now tied the label securely to Shep's collar.

'Home, Shep!' Peg commanded, and pointed the direction.

'Home, Shep!' Helen repeated, then wound up the window as Shep started off and the Doctor at last set his car in motion.

The track had been badly damaged by the storm: turf had been scoured away; banks of mud and loose stones lay along the route. At one stage the Doctor's car became bogged down in a hollow; whichever way he tried, forward or backward, wheel-spin only ploughed the car deeper.

Fortunately the Field Ranger was not far behind. The Chief Chemist skilfully manoeuvred it round the stranded car, then he produced a tow-rope from his tool kit, hitched it on to both vehicles, and with his four-wheel drive soon hauled the Doctor's car on to firm ground again. The two vehicles kept company until they reached Up-hill Farm.

19

At Up-hill Farm

In spite of confidence in their children's good sense, the Bairstow parents might have been anxious at the prolonged absence of the four children and two ponies during the cloudburst. This time Shep proved himself to be a reliable messenger. When he burst into the farm house barking and waving his tail, the label attached to his collar did not fail to receive attention. It was therefore no great shock to Mary Bairstow to see her daughter brought home in Doctor Hobday's car, wrapped in a car rug.

Little time was spent in explanations, but before Helen could go upstairs for a hot bath and change of clothing she had to lie on her back with her feet in the air while Mary eased off her waterlogged riding boots. Mary hurried off to keep an eye on the soup and make omelettes.

Christopher had been round the farm to assure himself that there was no storm damage requiring immediate attention. A wooden chicken-house had been caught by the rising water of the Up-hill Stream and had floated away but fortunately stranded again. The chickens were unharmed. Now he took off his streaming waterproofs in the back porch and greeted his visitors.

Colonel Savage had known Christopher since he was a boy and always called him by his first name. Now he introduced Derek Coleman and was sure enough of his identity to add that he was the Water Board's Chief Chemist. Then he indicated the stout man. 'Chris,' he said, 'can I ask you to find this man some hot water and dry clothes? We mustn't let him catch his death of cold. Doctor Hobday, may I trouble you to go along with our man and keep an eye on him? One other thing, Chris, if you please: may I use your telephone?'

'Certainly. It's through there in what I call my office.'

Christopher showed the way to the wash-house, where a sink and hot water were available, then went upstairs to seek a change of clothing for the stout man.

The Colonel found the telephone, lifted the hand-set and dialled, but the instrument was dead. He tried again, with no result, and came back to the Chief Chemist.

'I wanted to 'phone the Westover police to look out for a black sports car with my scoundrel of a nephew in it,' he said. 'He's mixed up in this business. But the line's dead. Water in the cables or wires down, no doubt.'

'That's easily dealt with,' Derek Coleman replied. 'You can send a message over my radio.'

They put on their raincoats again, went out and climbed into the cab of the Field Ranger. The Chief Chemist picked up his microphone.

'Water Speedwell calling Water Spider . . . Water Speedwell calling Water Spider. . . . Oh, hallo there. Derek Coleman speaking from out at Bincombe. We've had a devil of a rainstorm here; several inches, I should think. The telephone lines are out of order. I have Colonel Savage with me. He wants to pass a message to the Westover Police. I'll hand over to him.'

The Chief Chemist passed the microphone to the Colonel.

'Hello, there. I'd like you to take an urgent message for the Superintendent of Police at Central Police Station, Westover. Message begins: "From Colonel John Savage of Walden Lodge. Please intercept vintage black Perugi motor car, registration ALE 9876, and driver Gerontius d'Arcy, and hold for questioning. Probably making for London or a Channel port. Also send two officers to me at Mr Bairstow's, Up-hill Farm, Bincombe, to take another

142

man for questioning. Criminal charges may follow. Message ends." Now, please read that back over.'

He listened. 'Thank you. I'll hand you back to Mr Coleman.'

The Chief Chemist took the microphone again. 'You've got the message? . . . Good. Send it over as soon as you can. Water Speedwell over and out.'

The two men returned to the farm house.

By the time Peg had returned, watered the ponies, given them a bonus ration of oats and chaff, and turned them out to Five-acre, food was ready in the farm house. Mary had conjured up hot soup, toast, omelettes and fresh salad for all.

Christopher gave the Colonel a seat at the middle of the big oak table. He placed the stout man – now looking more cheerful, almost a figure of fun in cast-off clothing that was too long for him – opposite the Colonel, flanked by Derek Coleman on one side and Doctor Hobday on the other. Christopher himself and Mary sat at opposite ends of the table, with Helen near her mother to help with the serving. Peg, Robin and Adrian arranged their chairs at the remaining corners.

Helen had started to brew up hot milk coffee when there was a ring at the door bell. Adrian answered it. He saw a police car in the farm yard, and at the door stood a police sergeant and a constable – the very one that Adrian had encountered five weeks previously. Adrian grinned sheepishly.

'Police-Sergeant Pumphrey,' the first announced. 'And Constable Webber. There was a message from Colonel Savage asking us to come here.'

'You'd better come in,' Adrian said. Meeting the constable again was an embarrassment, but Adrian covered it by asking, 'Would you like some hot soup?'

'We would that,' was the reply. 'We've been out since seven this morning, with no time for a bite.'

The newcomers were ushered into the living-room, and chairs were placed for them on either side of the Colonel.

143

Adrian served up the last of the soup and Mary slipped away from the table to make more toast and omelettes.

Sergeant Pumphrey presently pushed back his empty bowl and wiped his moustache. 'They've pulled in the black Perugi and its driver,' he whispered in the Colonel's ear. 'We heard it on our radio. He was stuck in a low spot on the Market Lydford road with a waterlogged engine. Those low-slung sports cars catch it when there's too much water about. One of our patrols went to help and happened to notice his motor vehicle licence was out of date.'

The policeman buttered another piece of toast. Constable Webber was quietly enjoying Mary's omelette.

Helen brought in the coffee, and Adrian was helping her distribute cups round the table, when the Colonel spoke.

'There have been some unusual goings-on in what we call the Treacle Mine,' he said. 'And not only in the mine but round about. Some of us at this table know something of what has been going on, but not all of us yet know everything. As owner of the Walden Lodge estate I want all the facts.'

He looked straight at the stout man, who in order to drink his soup had turned up the cuffs of his concertina-like sleeves.

'You are Michael Scuser, are you not?' the Colonel asked. 'Otherwise known as Mick the Excuse.'

Everyone looked surprised, not least the stout man himself.

'I never forget a face,' the Colonel explained. 'I was chairman of the magistrates when you were committed to the Crown Court for trial on a charge of manslaughter. It was my last petty sessions before I retired. I remember your name because I asked you if you spelt it with a *c* or a *k*, and with an *s* or a *z*.'

Indeed the Colonel looked now as if he was presiding over a bench of magistrates.

144

'That affair was an accident,' Mick the Excuse protested.

'That is what you said at the time; but it was an accident that should never have happened. If you had not been drunk in charge of your motor vehicle the woman would never have been killed and the two policemen who tried to stop you would not have been badly injured. You have paid your penalty in a prison sentence, but it has not restored the dead woman to her husband and children.'

Colonel Savage looked round the table, then straight at the stout man again. 'You are a chemist, are you not?' he inquired.

'Chemical engineer,' Mick the Excuse corrected him.

'I suppose you got to know your accomplice Gerry d'Arcy when you were in prison.'

At this point Police-Sergeant Pumphrey put in a word. 'Excuse me, sir. I don't fully know why I have been asked to come here, but I gather that things have been happening that might lead to a criminal prosecution. So I should warn all of you present that anything that is said may be taken down and used in evidence.'

'Quite right, Sergeant,' said the Colonel.

Mick the Excuse looked sullen. 'I'm saying nothing,' he mumbled.

Constable Webber was already writing in his notebook.

Doctor Hobday chose this moment to lay something on the table in front of Colonel Savage. He carefully unfolded the handkerchief and revealed the pistol. The Colonel glanced at it, nodded, then looked round the table again and fixed his eyes on the Chief Chemist.

'Mr Coleman,' he said, 'I gather that some sort of chemical-making process has been going on in the Treacle Mine. You are a chemist of considerable experience, no doubt. What do you think would be the advantages of conducting such an enterprise in a hill cave like this?'

The Chief Chemist thought carefully before he replied. Then: 'Secrecy, I suppose. A plentiful source of clean water – very important, that. An easy way of disposing of liquid wastes – what are commonly called effluents – and possibly any batches of product that go wrong, as they well might in the early stages of production. In this case there is also a usable source of mechanical power from which electricity has been made. I am not sure about overhead costs, but I can see some obvious disadvantages, and I must say that on the whole the financial returns must be great to justify the effort expended.'

'My step-nephew got to know the Treacle Mine when he was in charge here. He could see what advantages it might offer. I notice he has even exploited the timber yard for fencing and other materials.' The Colonel again looked straight at the stout man in Christopher's oversize garments. 'Michael Scuser, what were you and my step-nephew, Gerry d'Arcy, making in the Treacle Mine?'

Mick the Excuse remained silent, so the Colonel turned again to the Chief Chemist.

'Mr Coleman, you yourself have now been into the Treacle Mine. Have you any idea what these two men – I say two, but there may be more – have you any idea what these men may have been making?'

'That is what I came out this morning to find out, but our inspection has been cut short, so I have been able to see very little. I too want to know because of the risk of polluting my Board's sources of water. We pride ourselves on taking great care of our water.'

'Have you no idea, then?'

'We may have a clue in something that happened at Bincombe Pool recently. Here, Adrian, you had better tell everyone.'

'It was early Tuesday morning,' Adrian recalled. 'We'd just arrived at Bincombe Pool to do some fishing, Robin and I, when all of a sudden the fish seemed to go mad. First they rushed about as if they were trying to get out of the water, then they rolled over, one by one, as though they were dead or drunk. I believe they may have recovered later. But there was a greyish cloud of something oozing

146

through the water. We tried to get some samples of it, and the Water Inspector took them to the Chief Chemist. I thought there might be some radioactivity, because of what the notice board says, but that was a mistake.'

The Chief Chemist took up the story again. 'I tested Adrian's samples for likely things that have been known to poison water – such as pesticides and salts of the heavy metals, lead and cadmium and so on – but the results were negative.'

The Colonel asked, 'So you found out nothing from Adrian's samples? No radioactivity?'

'No radioactivity. But next I tested for alkaloids, which are a large class of poisons derived from plants. It was a general test for alkaloids, not specific for any particular one of them.'

'And what did you find?'

'The result was positive: an alkaloid or alkaloids were present. Not a heavy concentration, but definite in both samples. I confirmed this with an alternative test.'

Doctor Hobday leaned forward. 'May I say a few words?' he asked.

'Yes, do,' was the Colonel's reply.

'I looked at Bincombe Pool this morning. I saw some trout there, lying in the water surface as if they were dead or drugged. But I would like to digress a little. Twice recently – on Tuesday morning and again this morning – a number of my patients have shown signs of a mysterious illness. At first I was puzzled; I thought it might even be an infectious disease. From my patients' symptoms I am now certain that it was a form of narcotic poisoning. The effects were like those of opium, whose constituents are, of course, alkaloids, which the Chief Chemist has just mentioned. I want to know if my patients have been affected by the self-same alkaloids as the Waterworks Chemist has detected in Adrian's samples from the Pool. If so, how can this have come about?'

From his breast pocket the Doctor drew out a large sheet of paper; he unfolded it and spread it on the

147

table.

'Go on,' said the Colonel.

'Those of my patients who have been affected have certain things in common. They are all early risers. They all start the day with one, two or even three cups of tea before going about their daily business; indeed, cups of tea seem to be a regular Bincombe habit. On both occasions – Tuesday and this morning – the illness came on after drinking their tea. I began to suspect the tea they put in the pot. But I found that it was bought at various places and was of different brands. I need not remind you that a cup of tea consists not only of packet tea, but also sugar, milk and water. I have found that a third of those affected do not take sugar in their tea; a few do not take milk.'

The Doctor paused to glance at his sheet of paper. He continued: 'I think we may eliminate sugar, milk and packet tea or tea bags from our inquiry. The other ingredient of cups of tea is water. All the patients have mains water – Walden Water Board water, Mr Coleman – and all live in the immediate vicinity of Bincombe village – very near to my own house, where the Up-hill lane joins the High Street. If mains water was the means of drugging my patients, how could a narcotic drug have got into the water main? And what was that drug?'

'I begin to see at least a partial explanation,' Derek Coleman replied. 'All the springs below Bradbury Castle on the north side of the hill are piped into a collecting chamber at the Meter House. We call them the Line of Springs. At the Meter House some of that water is chlorinated and passes into the main. The remainder flows over a weir and joins the headstream of the Bin Brook, which flows on down to Bincombe Pool. If an effluent got into the Line of Springs it would therefore affect both the water main and the fish pool.'

Doctor Hobday pursued his question: 'My patients were drugged, Adrian's fish were drugged. But why only on Tuesday morning and again this morning?'

The Chief Chemist replied, 'I suspect effluent from

148

what has been going on in the Treacle Mine. It is unlikely to have been constant, either in strength or quantity. Small-scale manufacture is likely to be a batch process; there might even be a batch or two discarded because the production had gone wrong or was not up to standard. If a large dose of effluent was discharged into the lake or a fissure at the Roman Cavern – large, that is, in strength or volume or even both – it might travel underground as a liquid mass, and pass as a brief slug of contaminated water along the Line of Springs to the Meter House. What was passed into the water there could continue as a slug down the pipe and be drawn off by your early risers; what overflowed to the brook would continue as a slug down to Bincombe Pool. Eventually such doses of effluent would become diluted and dispersed, so later you would find little or no trace of them.'

Colonel Savage returned to his original question. 'We need to know what was contained in the effluent. You have given us some idea. What we have to find out is precisely what was being manufactured. Michael Scuser, tell us, please, what you were making in the Treacle Mine.'

Mick the Excuse again remained silent. His face was rigid as a mask.

'When I was travelling in India and China,' the Colonel recalled, 'I sometimes saw opium poppies being grown. When ready, the poppy heads would be slashed and a milky juice would seep out. This was collected and dried in the sun to make the toffee-looking substance we call opium. Now, Mr Coleman, do you think the process being carried out in the Treacle Mine might be the next stage in the manufacturing programme – extraction of the drug morphine from crude opium?'

'I doubt it,' the Chief Chemist answered. 'I consider it more likely, judging by the apparatus we have seen and the vinegary smell, that the process was one stage farther on – that the process was conversion of the drug morphine, already extracted from opium, into the more powerful drug heroin. But, I must admit, this is little more than a

149

guess.'

Mick the Excuse allowed himself a sly grin.

For half a minute nobody spoke. Outside, rain continued to beat on the windows and tinkle in the gutters and downspouts.

Then, 'What about the wooden box?' Peg asked unexpectedly.

'What box is that?' demanded the Colonel.

'The box being nailed up in the Roman Cavern, ready for the Octopus on Sunday night. Adrian and I brought it out with us.'

Adrian got up hastily from the table and ran out to the yard. He was relieved to find the box still in the back of the Field Ranger and quickly brought it into the house, stopping only to pick up a pair of pincers and a stout screwdriver from the workshop. Slightly out of breath, and with raindrops in his hair, he placed the box on the polished table. Mary promptly found a newspaper and motioned to Adrian to lift the box while she inserted it underneath.

The box measured about eighteen inches in length, a foot wide and six inches deep. Its corners were neatly dovetailed and it bore the name of a well-known soapmaker.

The Colonel asked Adrian to prise off the lid. Adrian did so.

At this point Mick the Excuse jumped up anxiously as if to interrupt what was happening, then sat down again resignedly.

The interior of the box was lined with aluminium foil. Doctor Hobday, who was close to it, stood up and parted the lining, to reveal numerous small packets done up in more aluminium foil; there must have been a thousand of them neatly arranged in rows and layers. Each carried a stick-on label bearing an inscription in typewritten characters. Doctor Hobday bent closer to read it. 'The labels say,' he announced, ' "Detergent: Special formula".'

Detergent! Washing powder! Was that all it was, after all? Peg's face showed her disappointment.

The Doctor selected a packet, unfolded it and tipped out its contents on to his big sheet of paper, where it made a little heap of powder that looked in colour and texture like fine oatmeal.

Mick the Excuse could contain himself no longer. 'Steady on!' he cried. 'That packet's worth a grand.'

'If what you say is true,' Doctor Hobday snapped back at him, 'that boxful is worth at least a million pounds.'

'What is this stuff we are looking at?' Colonel Savage demanded.

Derek Coleman looked at the labels. 'We can soon see if it is detergent or not,' he suggested.

He picked up one of the coffee cups that were still on the table, went out to the kitchen and returned with a cupful of water. He dipped a forefinger into the water, then into the little heap of oatmeal-coloured powder, and rubbed forefinger and thumb together. He shook his head. Then he dipped his forefinger into the cup again and stirred it round vigorously. There was no frothing.

'I don't think it's detergent,' he announced.

The Colonel asked, 'Does anyone here know what this stuff is?'

There was silence. Then, 'I think it might be something called nerrowing,' Adrian said hesitantly.

The Colonel shifted his chair slightly to face him. 'What makes you say that?'

'We thought we heard something like *nerrowing* mentioned by the two men in the Treacle Mine when Robin and I went down there through the Swallock. But it might have been *narrowing*; it was difficult to hear what they were saying.'

Mick the Excuse glared at Adrian. If looks could kill, Adrian's life was in grave danger.

'Not *nerrowing* but *neroin*, perhaps,' Doctor Hobday suggested. 'I recognize the name *neroin*. Neroin is a drug. It's not often used in medical practice, and I must confess

151

I don't know much about it.' He turned to Derek Coleman.

'I've heard of neroin,' said the Chief Chemist, 'but I've never had anything to do with it.'

'Could you analyse it or test for it?' the Colonel asked him.

'It could be recognized and measured by high-performance liquid chromatography,' was the reply.

'Now you are blinding us with science,' the Colonel protested; but any rebuke in his voice was belied by his smile and a twinkle in his brown eyes.

'It's the sort of job that might be sent to the Government Chemist,' Derek Coleman hastened to explain.

The Colonel looked from face to face for inspiration. 'Can't anyone here add to what we seem to know about neroin?' he asked. He looked at Mick the Excuse, but the stout man only scowled and said nothing. There was another silence.

'It sounds like *heroin,* but with Nero instead of Hero,' the Colonel remarked.

Robin looked inquiringly at Helen, who decided she must speak out. 'That's just what it is,' she said. 'It's like heroin but different. I looked it up in *Klein's Dictionary of Applied Chemistry* at the Westover Central Library. The assistant there let me make a photocopy of the entry.'

Helen pulled a notebook from a pocket and took out a piece of paper that she proceeded to unfold.

'What does *Klein's Dictionary* say? Read it out,' the Colonel instructed.

Helen read out in a clear voice:

'NEROIN, a narcotic drug. It is similar to heroin, but has in its molecular formula an additional nitrogen (N) group in place of one of the hydrogen (H) atoms, hence the name *N*eroin. It was discovered in 1947 by the American pharmacologist Wilbur D. Schlesinger, who synthesized it from the juice of

Swedish turnips. It has been substituted for heroin in illegal drug trafficking, but besides having sedative and euphoric effects it is strongly addictive, and its persistent use can damage the retina of the eye and produce permanent blindness in its unsuspecting victims.'

The Colonel pushed back his chair from the table. 'We have seen and heard enough,' he said. 'Sergeant, I want you to take this man Michael Scuser to Westover Central Police Station for further questioning. As you know, his accomplice Gerontius d'Arcy is already there. I had better come along with you; there will be criminal charges to prepare.

'Constable, you had better take charge of this pistol and repack that box. Bring them along to the Central Police Station. We'd better bring Scuser's wet clothing as well.

'Mr and Mrs Bairstow, on behalf of all your visitors I thank you for your hospitality, which was very opportune. Your young people have been splendid; but more of that anon. Meanwhile I will leave my bicycle with you, if I may, and collect it in the next day or two.

'Doctor Hobday and Mr Coleman, we will keep in touch. The police may ask you for statements. Now, rain or no rain, we must be on our way.'

20

The Board meeting

Next day the weather was still unsettled, but bursts of sunshine alternated with overcast skies and restored everybody's good spirits.

Police-Sergeant Pumphrey rang up to say he was coming out to Up-hill Farm again, to take statements from Helen, Adrian, Robin and Peg. He was bringing Detective-Sergeant Badger with him, with the intention of seeing Mr Bairstow, and they both wanted to be sure everyone would be at home.

'We'd better sit round the big table again,' Christopher suggested when the two officers arrived.

'My uniformed colleague and I assumed we each had a separate jigsaw puzzle to solve,' the detective explained when they were all settled. 'But now the pieces are fitting into place we begin to see there are bits in common and it looks like one big jigsaw. There are still a few pieces missing, but not for long now.'

'Have you traced my stolen cattle?' Christopher asked anxiously. 'There are twenty-two pieces of jigsaw still missing so far as I'm concerned.'

'The short answer is yes, but there's more to it than that and a lot of police work still to be done.

'You'll remember I'd traced Peg's number plate to a car-breaker's yard near Hereford,' he continued. 'Well, I went there hoping to get more information about who acquired the number plates, but the breaker couldn't or wouldn't recall how he had disposed of them.

'Then I had some unexpected help that made my search a lot easier. When I asked the Hereford police if they recognized Denny's description of two cattle wagons, one a light-oak colour, the other a big one, dark blue with red lining, probably operating together, they seemed very interested. It turned out that there are two brothers who've been running a wholesale meat-supply business. Various misdemeanours have come to light – illegal slaughtering, for instance: a licensed slaughterhouse that was all above board, and up the mountain an unlicensed one that wasn't. There were other things: falsifying employees' earnings so as to reduce income-tax payments, insurance fiddles, giving short weight, etcetera. The wholesale meat-supply business suddenly received a lot of attention from various officials, and one discovery led to another. Now there are criminal charges pending.'

'And were the cattle wagons theirs?' asked Mary, who had been listening as keenly as the others round the table.

'Yes, there are two cattle lorries, used by the brothers, that fit Denny's description.'

Police-Sergeant Pumphrey now took up the story. 'Those wholesale-butcher brothers sound to me like petty crooks, and I emphasize petty. They're not very clever. They wouldn't have got themselves under suspicion all round if they'd had more sense. However, in the middle of our jigsaw is a piece that's still missing, and I think it carries a full-colour picture of a master criminal, someone who gets others to take the risks of criminal acts, while he keeps in the background and takes a nice rake-off from their activities. That's the person we've now got to lay hands on.'

'We've never seen anyone else with d'Arcy and Scuser,' Helen reflected.

'No, but our two did have some sort of hidden accomplice,' Adrian reminded her. 'Have you forgotten the Octopus?'

155

'Exactly,' Sergeant Pumphrey confirmed. 'The Octopus. Who is he, and where can we find him?'

Christopher Bairstow remembered something. 'Peter Gurney down at the filling station told me he'd seen another man in the shiny black car.'

'He was supposed to be a tick-tack man, wasn't he?' Sergeant Badger recalled. 'Often seen smoking a cigar?'

Peg asked, 'What is a tick-tack man?'

'A tick-tack man,' Christopher explained, 'is a bookmaker's scout. On a racecourse he goes round finding out what the jockeys and others are saying about the horses, and what odds other bookmakers are offering, and he signals these back to his employer, using his hands in a sort of semaphore called tick-tack.'

'It's scarcely a full-time occupation,' the detective continued. 'In this instance I reckon it's just a cover. Gerry d'Arcy brought this character hereabouts over the Treacle Mine business, and the fellow couldn't resist the opportunity to organise a bit of cattle rustling, but I guess he has several other rackets.'

'Not to mention distributing drugs to the pushers,' Police-Sergeant Pumphrey added. 'Now, you young people,' he went on, 'I want each of you in turn to tell me, as briefly as you can, what you have seen Gerontius d'Arcy and Michael Scuser actually doing and what you have heard them say. I will help you by asking questions but you mustn't speak too fast, because I want to write down what you tell me. It's all part of the process of preparing evidence to be used in a court of law.'

The policeman looked at Peg. 'First, Peg, it was you who told us that the box being nailed up in the Roman Cavern was to be ready for the Octopus on Sunday night. How did you know that?'

'That's what Robin told us. He and Adrian went down the Swallock, and they overheard the men talking in the Roman Cavern.'

Sergeant Pumphrey turned to Robin. 'You are Robin, aren't you? You'd better give me your full name, age and

156

address.'

Robin did as he was asked, and the policeman proceeded to write.

'Tell me about the Swallock and what you overheard in the Roman Cavern.'

Robin described Wednesday's descent with Adrian into the Swallock and their uncomfortable journey along the stream bed and into the tunnel until they came to the Roman Cavern.

'Lucky for both of you the cloudburst didn't happen till yesterday,' Sergeant Pumphrey commented. 'I'd be following up a different and very sad story if that storm had come Wednesday. But go on: what was it you heard the men saying?'

'There was a lot of noise in the Roman Cavern – water rushing, and the electric generator humming and an oil burner roaring – so we only caught snatches of what they said to one another.'

Robin went on to relate what he and Adrian had heard about keeping the pan stirred and the burner pumped up, about raising the lolly after being 'inside', and about expected payment in bank notes.

'Then one of them said – and I think it was the tall man, d'Arcy – "I rang the Octopus and told him we'd have the first lot ready for him on Sunday night, nine o'clock at old friends' where we met before." '

'Who are their old friends?' the policeman interrupted. 'And where can we find them?'

'That's what we wondered,' Helen put in.

'I can answer that,' Christopher told them. 'It's not old friends in the plural but old Friend in the singular with a capital F. Jack Friend was gamekeeper for the Colonel's father. He was an interesting old boy, remembered the Boer War and could tell all sorts of stories about Africa. He died just before Helen was born; it must have been while the present Colonel was away on his travels abroad and Gerry d'Arcy was in charge of the estate. I remember there was a hoo-ha about paying for the funeral; d'Arcy said the

157

estate wouldn't pay for it, so poor old Jack was laid to rest in Bincombe churchyard at public expense.'

'The question is not where is old Friend now, bless him, but where did he live?' Sergeant Pumphrey insisted.

'In the gamekeeper's cottage: down on the corner where the Up-hill lane meets the Market Lydford main road. That's what d'Arcy meant by old Friend's.'

'Right, we'll be there ready to catch the Octopus red-handed tomorrow night. Meanwhile I want to ask a few more questions. Adrian, have you anything to add to what Robin has told us? And I haven't heard yet what the girls can tell us. Meanwhile my colleague, Detective-Sergeant Badger, wants a word with Mr Bairstow.'

The policeman went on questioning the cousins while the detective talked to Christopher at the other end of the big table.

'Mr Bairstow,' said Sergeant Badger, 'I've drafted a short statement for you, based on what you've already told me. I want you to read it carefully. If there's anything not quite right, or not how you would have put it, I want you to tell me and we'll amend it. Then, when you agree it's correct, I shall ask you to sign it and initial any alterations. What is more, I would like you to hold yourself ready to attend court, if you are so requested, to give evidence about your stolen cattle.'

'When and where will that be?' Christopher asked.

'It's too early yet to be certain. I expect the case will be tried at Westover, but it might be heard at Hereford or elsewhere because of other charges against the accused. If all goes well you may have to make arrangements at short notice for transporting your cattle back to Bincombe.'

On the following Tuesday it was Peg, of course, who discovered that the kittens' eyes were open. She was already making plans for taking at least one of Esmeralda's offspring back home with her when she and

Robin returned at the end of the holiday. Mary warned her that they would not be weaned and sufficiently developed to leave their mother until they were eight weeks old. So much had happened in the past ten days, said Peg, it seemed that the kittens might have been born a whole month ago.

'But I would like to have the black one,' she added. 'He's going to be just like Anthracite.'

'You could come and collect him at mid-term,' Mary suggested.

No word had come from Police-Sergeant Pumphrey or Detective-Sergeant Badger, but a brief announcement in the morning news bulletin said that narcotic drugs 'with a street value of two million pounds' had been seized by Customs officials 'at a farm in the Walden Hills'; details could be expected later.

Now that the floods had subsided, and the fields had started to dry out sufficiently for people and animals to move about without slipping or becoming caked in mud, everyone at Up-hill Farm was mobilized to move the chicken house to a suitable new position. Christopher Bairstow directed the operation, Adrian was again allowed to drive the tractor (with wry jokes, at his expense, about flattening fences), and the rest used bricks and fencing stakes to lever the wooden structure along gently whenever it got stuck and was in danger of being torn apart by Adrian's tow-ropes. Finally Danny demonstrated his great strength by picking up each end of the chicken house bodily, in turn, to place it on the new footings. He seemed none the worse for having twice been drugged with neroin.

The cloudburst had laid low much of the corn, but fortunately Christopher had only a small acreage under barley and oats that year, and a spell of fine weather following the heavy rainfall enabled him to save much of it, though it was difficult work. He himself did not own a combine harvester, but he helped his neighbours at Binbrook Farm to harvest their crops and they brought a

159

harvester and helped him. Danny, Adrian and Robin also assisted throughout. Robin was fascinated by the machinery, and towards the end of operations he was allowed, under their neighbours' supervision, to try his hand at driving the combine harvester. This again brought forth some sly jokes, but it made his day.

Bincombe Flower Show and Gymkhana loomed only two weeks away. Helen entered herself in the riding section and Peg in the beginners' class. Under Helen's direction, Adrian and Robin built pony jumps in Five-acre, and for a while the two girls spent much of each day on pony-back.

The two boys resumed their visits to Bincombe Pool. No dead fish were found; indeed, the trout once again seemed lively and greedy for mayflies, real or artificial. Adrian asked for and obtained permission to use the dinghy on the Pool whenever he wished, and with a solemn warning from the angling club secretary about rocking the boat he was given a key to the padlock and told where the plug was hidden. Now he and Robin were able to try other techniques of angling. At Up-hill Farm, trout became a regular variant of the menu.

When the great day came, judging in the flowers and produce marquee was all done by midday, and results were announced over a loudspeaker system rigged up by Sparky Harris. Mary Bairstow was awarded first prize for six single-yolk hen eggs, brown, and firsts for three vases of garden flowers, distinct varieties, and three pots of jam, all one sort. Christopher Bairstow took prizes for the best six swedes, the best three kale and the best six carrots, short horn, but he failed to win the prize for the largest marrow in the Show, which went to Danny. Peg Gaskell took first prize for the best vase of wild flowers (children 10 to 16 years).

The riding events came in the afternoon. Helen was doing well in the under 14·2 hands jumping, when Grimaldi collected three faults for a refusal. 'He would play the fool just at that moment,' she lamented. But a few minutes later her nearest rival had a similar misfortune, and in the jump-off against the clock Grimaldi pricked up his ears and went clear. Both in the beginners' class (children under 14 years) and for the best-turned-out pony, Peg was highly commended.

In the days that followed there were picnics on the Walden Hills and excursions to the coast, where the sun had warmed the sea sufficiently to persuade even Christopher to go swimming. Then Adrian and Robin had another trip to the coast, this time with Sparky Harris and his friends, to take part in a day's boat fishing. They started early in the morning to catch the tide and returned late in the evening with an assortment of flounders, plaice, bass, pollack and – the source of great excitement when it was caught – a conger. Robin reflected that the holiday had not worked out too badly after all.

The telephone had long since been restored when one morning there was a ring. 'It's the Water Board asking for Miss Helen Bairstow,' said Mary, handing the 'phone to her daughter.

'Good morning,' said a now familiar voice. 'This is the Walden Water Board office, and it's Derek Coleman, Chief Chemist, speaking. Are your cousins still with you? . . .

'Fine. Well, now, the Water Board holds a quarterly meeting the first week in September, and our Chairman would like you to come along and be thanked for what you did at the Treacle Mine. It's next Thursday. Can you make it? . . .

'Your cousins are going home next day, you say. . . .

'The meeting starts at ten o'clock, but it usually ends by eleven, when the members have a cup of coffee before dispersing. Can all four of you come along here on Thursday, then, at eleven o'clock?'

Helen said they could, and he rang off.

As it happened, the day and time suited Christopher, for it was his market day. When the occasion arrived he put all four down by the Walden Water Board office and arranged to meet them later at the car park.

At the Water Board's reception desk the Chief Chemist came to greet them.

'It's Sir Keith Adamson in the chair,' he said, and ushered them into the Board room. 'Mr Chairman, please let me present Miss Helen Bairstow, her brother Adrian, their cousin Robin Gaskell and his sister Miss Peg Gaskell.'

'Come and sit down,' said the Chairman. 'There are some seats here. Would you like coffee? Or would you prefer tea or orange juice? Help yourselves to biscuits.'

He himself took another biscuit and pushed back his empty coffee cup.

'We are glad you have come along this morning,' he went on, 'because we want to thank you for averting a serious threat to our water supplies. Mr Coleman, our Chief Chemist, has told me the whole story. By your alertness, and your careful reasoning, and your courage in following up clues, you managed to resolve a problem that might have defeated us for a long time.'

Helen began to feel embarrassed. Peg wanted to giggle. The two boys listened stolidly as the Chairman continued.

'I don't know much about neroin. I understand that such drugs can be a blessing if properly administered to people in pain, but in the wrong hands they can lead to drug dependence, ill health and worse. I am told that addicts crave for such drugs, and if they have no money to buy them they fall into extreme poverty and steal to pay the drug-pushers. So in detecting the illegal manufacture of this drug you have not only done the Water Board a good turn, but have helped governments all over the world, Customs officers, the police, doctors and social workers, who are striving to stamp out a world-wide criminal traffic that endangers health.

'To show our appreciation we wish to give you something tangible. Miss Helen, I have heard that you intend to become a journalist. We have therefore decided that a suitable present would be a portable typewriter, and

162

here it is.'

The Chairman stood up and whisked the cover from a brand-new typewriter standing on the Board-room table. He seized Helen by the hand and shook it. Board members sitting around the table applauded. Helen was so surprised that she could do little more than murmur, 'Oh, thank you. Thank you very much indeed' – which after the Chairman's speech was probably better than a lengthy response.

'Miss Peg,' Sir Keith continued, 'a little bird tells me that you would like to have a luminous date watch like your brother's. Well, here it is. Let me put it on for you.'

Peg held out her left wrist while he strapped the watch on. Then he warmly shook her right hand. 'Tell me,' he asked, 'what do you intend to do when you grow up?'

Like Helen, Peg began to feel embarrassed, but after a slight hesitation she replied, 'Well, sir, I would like to have a riding school, and to teach people how to ride and how to look after horses and ponies. Thank you very much for such a lovely present.'

It was Adrian's turn next, and for him the Chairman had a reflex camera. In presenting it Sir Keith asked what Adrian intended to do when he left school.

'I hope to go on to an agricultural college, and I expect I shall become a farmer, like my father and grandfather,' Adrian replied. 'Thank you very much for the reflex camera. It is something I have wanted, and will use and cherish.'

Now it was Robin's turn. 'For you,' the Chairman announced, 'we have a pair of field glasses.' He handed the binoculars and their case to Robin and shook hands with him. 'And what do you want to become some day?'

'Thank you, sir,' Robin replied. 'I like doing things in the open air, and a pair of field glasses is a most useful present. I have always wanted to be an engineer, but lately I have thought I would like to be an explorer.'

'Why not combine the two and become, say, a mining engineer?' Sir Keith suggested. 'Much of the world has already been mapped, but the future will demand exploration and exploitation of fuels and other mineral wealth underground and under the seas. You might even develop your own treacle mine!'

'I shouldn't like that,' was Robin's ready answer. 'I've been down the Swallock, and I was very glad to get out again.'

Robin seemed to be enjoying the situation. An impish grin spread across his face. He cleared his throat. Peg feared he was about to say something silly.

'Even with binoculars,' he declared, 'I cannot expect to be very far-sighted. But my thoughts on what you suggest sound like a Chinese proverb: "People who dabble in treacle mines will come to a sticky end." '

AUTHOR'S POSTSCRIPT

The events I have described took place at a time when a new Act of Parliament, intended to curb the appalling traffic in addictive drugs, had only recently come into operation. A year later the Walden Water Board, which figured in our story, lost its identity in a reorganization of the water industry. So much for history.

Readers may wonder if Christopher Bairstow finally got his cattle back and what has since happened to the people in our story.

Helen has become a successful journalist and feature-writer; she is engaged to marry a doctor. Adrian obtained a diploma at his agricultural college and will probably take over Up-hill Farm when Christopher and Mary retire.

Christopher meanwhile bought Magpie Ground from Colonel Savage. When the Colonel died at a ripe old age the remainder of the Walden Lodge estate was acquired by a syndicate, and Adrian has been appointed manager, responsible for revitalizing the farm land and woods while conserving the estate's natural amenities – truly (ahem!) an 'Up-hill' task, as Robin has not failed to comment. The Treacle Mine has been made safe by reinforcing the natural roof in the Western and Eastern Adits and walling-off the maze-like side passages. Electric lighting has been extended, and the Roman Cavern is now a popular tourist attraction that brings in some profit to pay for conservation elsewhere on the estate.

Robin has become an associate in a firm of consulting engineers with world-wide connections, so is able to follow his desires for both engineering and travel. Peg has become a Lecturer in Botany at one of the technological universities, so is teaching about plants, not ponies, though she is still a keen and active rider. Her black kitten has become a big cat but retains the lithe beauty inherited from Esmeralda and Anthracite. Shep has died of old age but has been succeeded at Up-hill Farm by a similar black-and-white Border collie.

Police-Sergeant Pumphrey and Constable Webber had no difficulty in tracing the Octopus. As expected, he was the tick-tack man. The Superintendent of Police at Westover instructed them to collaborate with officers of Customs & Excise to set a trap for the Octopus, using the vintage Perugi as a decoy and the wooden box of so-called detergent as a bait. The Octopus was arrested as he emerged from old Friend's cottage carrying the box of neroin. The policemen discovered he had a hide-out where other narcotic drugs were warehoused. The Octopus had previously served a term in prison for drug-trafficking, and it was there he had got to know d'Arcy and Scuser and planned what they might do when they were let out. Now he was given a further sentence and heavily fined for contravening the new Drugs Act. But that was not all.

It was while he was in prison on the previous occasion that the Octopus had got to know one of the brothers who ran the wholesale meat-supply business, also doing time in gaol. So it was the Octopus who master-minded the cattle robbery and instructed the brothers where to find Christopher's cattle unattended. The brothers were sent to prison for that affair, and the Octopus was convicted with them and given a further sentence. Christopher recovered his beef cattle in time to send them to market when prices were rising for the Christmas season; but Detective-Sergeant Badger never did trace the other two full-mouthed cows, for which Christopher had to be content with a payment of compensation from his insurers.

Gerontius d'Arcy and Michael Scuser were charged and

convicted under the Drugs Act, and also for motor-vehicle and firearms offences. They too were given prison sentences, but subsequently earned some remission for good behaviour. Soon after he came out of gaol this time d'Arcy succeeded in finding and marrying a rich widow; he now spends his time *dolce far niente* on the Italian riviera. Mick the Excuse underwent treatment for his alcoholism and – surprise! – has become a reformed character. Robin encountered him recently in Africa, where Mick is using his undoubted ingenuity and energy in a beneficial way: by helping a well-known relief organization to show undeveloped peoples how to overcome drought and famine.